The Spirit of Jem

P. H. NEWBY

with illustrations by

KEITH VAUGHAN

LONDON

JOHN LEHMANN

1947

FIRST PUBLISHED IN 1947 BY
JOHN LEHMANN LTD
MADE AND PRINTED IN GREAT BRITAIN
BY PURNELL AND SONS LTD
PAULTON (SOMERSET) AND LONDON

FOR
SARAH JANE

CONTENTS

PART ONE

CHAPTER I

SOMETHING TO BE REMEMBERED

I DID NOT know where I was.

I had awakened, it seemed, to a bright afternoon. No matter in what direction I looked I could see rolling hill country neatly divided up by grey stone walls. Here at my feet, for I was standing at a point where the lane was crossing a ridge so that I was raised above the surrounding country, was a field quite white with daisies. Purple clouds were going along the horizon. Where was I? Never in my life before had I seen this lane nor this field of daisies; yet even as I looked at them they nagged at my memory as though I had previously seen them in a dream. I found that my legs were trembling but this was not with fear. Although I could not remember it I knew that I had been running for my heart was beating against my ribs and the perspiration was getting cold on my forehead. My legs trembled because they could carry me no farther and I sat down on a small boulder at the side of the road. I was really too tired to be very much alarmed but there were all sorts of thoughts in my head, all sorts of questions to be answered,

9

that sent vibrating currents through my body like gentle electricity.

What had I seen that had made me run, for obviously I had been running away from something? And how could I run out of a place that I knew into what seemed a different world? I had never seen purple clouds before nor a field quite so brilliantly white with daisies. Even as I tried to make my brain work another terrible thought struck me. What did I mean by the world that I knew? For I was suddenly horrified to realise that I could remember no other world but this. Although the rolling fields between their grey walls looked so strange, I could not, for the moment, remember any other countryside. I had lost my memory. I was lost, terribly lost.

I suddenly sprang up and looked at the stone on which I had been sitting. It was perfectly black and highly polished. It winked in the sun as though thousands of tiny mirrors had been set in its surface but what struck the eye particularly was a terrible red gash in its side as though the stone had been charged with living blood and someone had given it a murderous slash with a sword. I was so troubled by my own thoughts that I could not bring myself to look at the stone calmly and quietly and it was only later that I discovered that it was nothing more than a piece of bright sandstone which someone had coated with tar. But I could not look at anything calmly for another painful thought had come to me.

Who was I ? Yes, in addition to not knowing where I was I did not know who I was.

I looked down at my clothes. My shoes were old and cracked as though they had never seen polish, my grey stockings had holes in the side, my knees looked red as though they had been whipped by a cold wind, but my grey, short trousers were clean and decent. I clapped a hand to my backside and found an enormous patch there. I was wearing a grey woollen jersey, also plentifully patched, and under that a grey shirt. Whoever I was, I wasn't particularly wealthy.

All my past life had been obliterated and it gave me a feeling of standing on the edge of nothing, like a man on the edge of a great cliff but standing with his back to it. He cannot see the great gulf behind him but there is a sense of emptiness behind, a whirling of the wind, a great pressing up of air. And so it was with me. I was young, about twelve or thirteen, but it seemed that the years I had lived were lying behind me and if I were not careful I should fall back and fall back. . . .

The air was thrilling with a little tune. There was no moment when the music began but only a moment when I said, " There are skylarks," knowing that they had been there all the time and I had not heard them. It was the same kind of high, thin trilling, but the sound was too close at hand, coming from too near the ground to be a skylark. And it was a tune, a definite tune that could be sung. I looked round me, so delighted with the music that I only remembered my painful thoughts to say, " It is a dream and soon I shall wake up."

The whistling, it seemed to me, was coming from the other side of the stone wall that ran alongside the edge of the road. I stepped on the grass and put my hands on top of the wall for it was just about the height of my chest. The whistling was very close now. Selecting a place for my toe, I levered myself on to the top of the wall, looked over and almost fell back again in surprise.

Sitting among the daisies was a plump, elderly gentleman, wearing a bowler hat and playing on the sort of tin

whistle you hold in your mouth like a stick of barley sugar while you let your fingers dance over a number of small holes down its length. The plump gentleman was blowing out his cheeks, quite red and rosy like ripe apples, and a large brown moustache trembled under his nose. But the extraordinary thing was that he was wearing no trousers, at least not the sort of long, respectable trousers that a gentleman of his kind would normally wear. He was wearing what looked to me like white football shorts.

"Eh! What's this I'd like to know?" I suddenly found that the music had stopped and the gentleman was looking at me with a pained expression on his face. "Don't you like music, or what? That's what I'd like to know?" All the time he had been holding his whistle in the air in front of him so as to lose no time when he wanted to continue. His voice was deep and pleasant. "Just found this in my pocket," he said, nodding at the whistle. "Well, if you want to listen, come in and sit down."

' Come in' was a queer way of inviting you to climb over a wall I thought but nevertheless I scrambled over, for I suddenly realised that I was very glad of the gentleman's company. He waited for me to settle myself among the daisies and then began to play once more. I could now tell that he was not playing at all well. His fingering was clumsy and he got short of breath rather easily so that he was forced to stop and fill his lungs. But the tone of the whistle itself was so sweet that I imagine it would have been impossible to make an unharmonious sound with it.

"Here," he said, "you have a try." He tossed the whistle over with the sort of disgusted expression on his face that said he had had enough of it.

"But I don't know how to play."

"Neither do I, neither. You wouldn't be trying to flatter me, would you? " He gave me a shrewd look and stretched out his legs with a sigh. But before I could put the whistle to my mouth he had shot another question at me.

"What's your name? "

I felt very foolish but I had to say that I did not know. He did not seem at all surprised and this encouraged me to the extent that I was able to answer the rest of his questions in quite an ordinary tone of voice. He wanted to know where I came from and what I was doing in this part of the world. Eventually I said I thought I must have lost my memory.

"I expect you think this is all a dream? " he asked.

"It seems like that." And then, quite bold now, "How long does a dream last? "

"All your life," said the gentleman after a pause and looked round among the daisies as though he had lost something. "That is, some dreams do. But this isn't what you could call a dream, is it? Look around for yourself, boy. Pick a daisy! Rub your knees! Solid, ain't they? Yes, it's darned queer, that's what I say. You've never had a dream as solid as this, have you? I never have."

"But *you're* not dreaming. Perhaps you're only in my dream."

"And it's just as likely you're something in a dream I'm having. No, son, we're not going to get to the bottom of this mystery by talking about dreams. This is different."

He got to his feet, slowly and painfully as though he had been sitting there a long time. He left a round patch of crushed daisies. "Look at that, for example, does it seem normal for a responsible gentleman like myself to be walking about with no trousers on?"

"No," I said.

"That's what I mean to say. It's a mystery and between you and me I'm beginning to suspect foul play. . . ."

He must have noticed my surprise.

"Yes, foul play. I think you and me's been victimised, set upon, made a mock of and what is more, robbed!"

"What do you mean?" I asked.

"This is what I mean. You don't know who I am and what's more I don't know who I am, either. You've never seen me in your life before and if it comes to that, I've never seen myself in my life before. I don't know who I am and that's the short of it, young man."

"Do you mean that you've lost your memory, too?"

"Young man, I do. And what I want to know is this. Why?"

There was a troubled, gentle expression on his face. He looked so ridiculous standing there in his football shorts that I had to struggle with myself to avoid laughing. Not so very much before I had been scared and bewildered. Now I wanted to laugh. It was, of course, comforting to find somebody suffering from the same complaint. He looked so solid and respectable that it was unimaginable that anything could be seriously wrong. I only had to remain with him and the extraordinary situation would be sorted out in no time.

"So you think it's funny, do you?" He put the tin whistle back in the breast pocket of his coat. "Have you seen anybody else about? No, not a soul, I thought not."

As I have explained, we were in a commanding position and if there had been a town or other inhabited place in the neighbourhood we should have seen the smoke going up from the chimneys. But there was no smoke. We looked around. There were no labourers in the fields, no 'planes in the sky. We might have been alone in the world. What if the end of all living people on the face of the earth had come and we, this gentleman and myself, by some fantastic chance, had been left as the only survivors?

The green hills bulged out of the earth like muscles; I could pick out a line of trees in the valley below and the purple clouds on the horizon were now swelling like cheeks. But everything was as silent as an empty house. There was not even a groove in the earth to tell of a plough. An exciting thought that we were alone, so exciting in fact that I forgot the gentleman and began considering just what can be done with the world when you have it all for your own. I could pillage the cities, I could take what I wanted from the great shops, the sweetmeats from the confectioners, the cars from the garages, the treasure from the vaults of the banks. I was Emperor for that moment. And then a wind blew in my face and the old question came back to me, " But who am I? Where am I? Who am I? "

In that moment I could see what it would be like walking through the deserted streets of a dead city listening to my own hollow footsteps.

There was a cough, a well-controlled cough that showed the gentleman wanted to be polite. " This is," he said, " when all is said and done, embarrassing. All alone in a strange place with no proper trousers to wear—all alone with you, that is to say, young man."

" What if everybody's dead? What if there is nobody else? "

" This is the most extraordinary dream I have ever had in my life," he said, shaking his head. "At least, I should imagine it is because I don't remember having had any other dreams. The best thing we can do is to go and explore. That is to say, investigate. That is to say, we must take our bearings. Don't be frightened, young man. We may be surrounded by enemies but trust in me. Have courage." And he scrambled over the stone wall. I followed. We walked along the road and he gave me grave instructions about what we must do if we met anybody. He explained that we were in a very difficult situation and if it was not a dream then we were both running a very grave risk of being locked up in a lunatic asylum.

" I know who you are, anyway," he said.

" Oh? "

" You're Roger."

" How do you know? "

" Because you look like a Roger."

" What is that like? "

" All Rogers look like Rogers. You've noticed that, though. When you've seen one Harry, you've seen all of them. They all run to type. I can pick Berts, Freds and Willies for you out of a crowd, just by looking at them. You're a Roger."

" Roger what? "

" Ah! I can't tell you that, though. Not yet. I'd have to see your teeth for that. It's an interesting point, though." He pushed out his lower lip and blew his moustache out as he considered matters. " Why were they called Rogers to begin with? Why were they called Toms? Why is a horse called a horse? Because they look like horses or Toms or Rogers, you see, young man."

All the time we were walking towards a great shadow that hung over the valley now that the sun began to go down.

"And that brings me to another point," he continued comfortably. " You were asking who you were. Now that's not important. What is important is this. Why are you? "

" Why am I? "

" Yes, why are you you and not me? And why am I me and not you? And why are either of us us? Why aren't you that stone and where does the stone begin and you end? Eh? "

" I don't understand what you are talking about."

" We've got to look out for strange things, that's what I mean to say, and I've got to give you a strict warning. Better let me do all the talking."

" But there's nobody to talk to. I don't know who I am. That's what worries me," I complained as we began to descend a hill. " Look at these hills all the way round."

For the hills were swelling larger around us as we went into the hollow. "They've shut us in altogether. I can't imagine anything going on behind those hills. It's terribly lonely just here."

"Sh!" said the gentleman suddenly. "Look." He pointed with his hand and I could see a signpost standing at a crossroads. "You mark my words, young man, something will happen when we get there."

"How do you know something will happen?"

"Because it looks just the sort of place for something to happen, doesn't it? Just you wait and see what is written on that signpost." We both fixed our eyes upon the neat white post with its two arms looking rather as though they had been cut out of cream cheese.

"There's nothing on it," I said in some alarm as we came up to it. It was as though everything were conspiring against us, taking our memories away from us and now not even permitting a signpost to give us some hint to our mysterious surroundings. In my eagerness I had hurried on in front. I came up to the white signpost and looked up at the arms. I could now see that there were two words, scribbled in what appeared to be red ink on the signpost, one on each arm. The left arm bore the word 'Yes' and the right arm bore the word 'No.'

"Yes and No," I called back to my companion.

"Either there is or there isn't," he said. "No half and half." And he screwed up his eyes to gaze at the words written there while I felt my heart sink, thinking that there was a sinister meaning behind the two words which we should soon discover.

One of the things I noticed about the adventures that we went through was that there were periods of doubt when the uncertainties of our position seemed to rob me of power

18

of thinking; and then there were periods when it seemed we went on in blithe confidence. It was like the swing of a pendulum, backwards and forwards, or the coming and going of the tide. From the time when I had become aware of my loss of memory up to the moment when I read the words ' Yes ' and ' No ' on the signpost, I think I shall call my first period of Not-Knowing. With the arrival of a new figure on the scene we slipped into a period of Knowing; but you will see that what I came to know was very little indeed.

The gentleman and I were aware of a sound above our heads that was neither whistling nor singing but a suggestion of both. I was immediately reminded of the tin whistle. My companion made the same mistake as I had made.

" It's larks," he said, looking up at the sky.

" More like to be a tin whistle," I said.

" Or a bagpipe."

" No, it's a fire." I was more emphatic this time for it could definitely be classed as a bell of some description. There was a shout and we looked up the road that the signpost said led to No. A man on a white box-tricycle bearing the words, " Mather's Pork Sausages " was bearing down on us at such a rate that a plume of white dust rose behind him, curled into the air like mist and shut out the distance.

" Out of the way," the man on the tricycle shouted as he flashed past, the machine obviously out of control, for he was holding his feet in the air, his knees up to his nose and the pedals were whirling beneath him.

" I told you something would happen when we got here," said Bowler Hat. " He'll stop in a moment. That hill will stop him. He won't get very far up there."

About fifty yards up the hill the machine came to a stop and the man hopped from the saddle and sat down at the side of the road with his head in his hands.

"Perhaps he's hurt," I suggested.

"No, he'll be down in a moment, I think. I know that fellow. Something tells me I've seen him before." He wrinkled his brow as he thought and I, as anxious as he was to stir up faltering memory, plied him with details of the stranger's dress and appearance that I had noticed as he had flashed past. "He had red hair and was wearing bicycle clips."

Bowler Hat shook his head. "No, it's no good. We'll have to wait until he comes back."

We had been so busy talking that we had taken our eyes off the tricyclist and when we looked for him he had already covered half the distance between his tricycle, which he had left behind, and us. Sure enough, his hair was red but the dust of the road had settled on him like flour so that he might have been a miller. But he was a plump, round-faced fellow and when he came up to us he stuck his hands in his pockets and whistled shrilly out of the corner of his mouth.

"Want a fight?" he asked me politely. "I don't suppose you do though. I can fight anybody. Who are you?" He turned to my companion and stared at his football shorts. In everything that he did there was the greatest self-assurance and almost a contempt that he could not be bothered to hide. I thought that he could not be very much older than I. But the very fact that he was so positive and self-confident did me good I think. He was taking control of the situation. He looked back at me and examined my dress minutely from head to toe. "Well, you've got yours on. Hey! They must be yours."

"What?" said my friend in the bowler hat, because it was to him that the newcomer had spoken.

"Trousers. They must be your trousers. I've got 'em. I found them on a scarecrow at the top of the hill. Leastways, I call it a scarecrow, though it was only a few sticks tied together. It hadn't any clothes on save the trousers. I thought it looked odd. So I took them and put them in the box. Up there. Have a cigarette?"

He appeared to be asking himself for he looked at neither Bowler Hat nor me but fumbled in the inside pocket of his jacket. He drew out a brown leather wallet, opened it and showed us the cigarettes it contained. "I found 'em," he explained. "I put my hand in my pocket just as I did then and there it was. Easy as picking up a penny. And in this pocket was a bit of string and the photo of a horse. No money, though. I even went through the lining."

While he was talking, Bowler Hat was whispering fiercely in my ear. "Don't trust that chap. It's a trap. How did he get hold of my trousers, that's what I'd like to know. He's not on our side." Then noticing that the stranger had lit his cigarette and was quietly watching us, he pushed his lips up against my ear and murmured, "I reckon he's in league with them."

"In league with whom?" I wanted to ask but the plump stranger was quivering with laughter. "What is it you want?"

"My trousers."

"There, what did I tell you?" said Bowler Hat out loud, staring at the newcomer quite boldly. "It's all a trap. Just ask him what those words on the signpost mean and find out."

"Oh, I dunno," said the stranger immediately. "I don't suppose it's of any importance."

We had forgotten all about the purple clouds that had lined the southern horizon but now it was as though someone had drawn a great sword in the sky and the declining sun had sent a flash along its polished steel. There was a heavy rolling and grating, and looking up we saw that the purple clouds were over our heads and we were caught, without any sign of shelter, in a sudden thunderstorm. We saw the white dust of the roadway turned to mud; felt our hair dragged clumsily down over our foreheads; heard a noise in our ears like heavy gunfire. The stranger plucked my sleeve and set off at a run with his head down, his shoulders hunched up to keep the rain from running down his neck. He had not said a word but I felt suddenly glad that something had been decided for me and raced after him, splashing through the puddles that had miraculously appeared already. I could just see the stranger's dim form as through a gauze curtain, some distance ahead of me. Then I lost sight of him until I heard him call and turned to see him clamber over a stone wall and go climbing up a grassy bank. I had barely reached the wall when the rain stopped as unexpectedly as it had begun and the whole world, grey walls, and green slopes, were electrically bright as the new sunlight caught the raindrops.

Then I saw the roof of the cabin. It was only a moment's walk from the crossroads but Bowler Hat and I had not been able to see it. It was tucked away in a grassy cleft with a silver birch tree outside the front door. There was a large, glittering axe leaning against the tree and I thought it would be just like the stranger to want to cut it down. He came to the front door as I reached the cabin and asked me where my friend was. I had completely forgotten about him.

"Ah—he'll have gone to get his trousers," said the stranger.

22

" Well——? " He stood there in the doorway smiling at
me. There was something in his eye that told me he knew
all about me, where I came from, my name, who my
parents were, what I was doing in this part of the
country.

" How do you feel? " he asked, in what I thought was a
very kindly way.

" You know that we've lost our memories, me and my
friend."

" I've lost my memory, too," said the stranger. " There
are a great many of us round here and you'll be meeting
us all shortly. It is part of a great plan to destroy us and
the world. We are surrounded by enemies." As he spoke
the smile faded from his face and was replaced by a look
of defiance as though his enemies were at that moment in
front of him.

23

"What enemies? I don't understand."

"The only way we can overcome them is by courage. We are fighting a merciless foe." His voice was metallic.

Already the heat of the sun was causing a mist to rise on the wet grass. The words of the stranger had filled me with exultation. In some strange way they had spoken to an inner part of me. My blood was stirred as though a trumpet had called.

"Think about what you have remembered," said the stranger. "Do not try to remember what you have forgotten."

I did not understand but his words made me forget the fact that I was soaked to the skin.

"What is your name?" I asked.

"You can call me Jem," he replied briefly. He was now as tense as a piece of steel in great contrast with the cocksure playfulness with which he had first greeted us. "Now, let's go and look for that fool."

We found Bowler Hat standing under the signpost with the box-tricycle which, apparently, he had wheeled down the road. I was too embarrassed to look at him, feeling how strongly he resented my having deserted him. Without a word the stranger drew a key out of his pocket, unlocked the box and threw back the lid. He dragged a pair of trousers out by one of the legs and whirled them round his head.

"I've got lots of things in here," he said, but he snapped the lid down too quickly for me to get a look inside.

Bowler Hat had been examining his trousers carefully. He was disgusted with them, that was evident. "It is quite obvious to me, young man," he said to the stranger, "that these garments are not mine. See, this great patch. I would

24

never have consented to wear things like this. However, under the circumstances . . ." and he slipped them on. Jem watched him, a little smile playing over his lips.

"I tell you those are your trousers and if you don't like them you can leave them. But come on up to the cabin. We must get warm. We're all soaked."

Altogether, Jem was a mysterious person. He slipped from a mood of light playfulness into a mood of steely hardness. I suppose he was thinking of his enemies just then —our enemies, that is to say, for Jem had made it quite clear that he and I were on the same side. . . . The sun was setting and soon it would be dark. We managed to lift the box-tricycle over the wall and push it up the grassy slope to the cabin, for there did not appear to be any proper path. It was just possible to push the tricycle in through the front door and no sooner had we done so, than Jem slammed the door closed and pulled down a great wooden bar. I could hear the bar grating down but not see it. The darkness was so intense that it almost hurt the eyes and pinpoints of white light seemed to dance on the very eyeballs. We might have been standing in some limitless cavern. When Jem struck a match and cupped it in his hands so that our three black shadows danced and grimaced on the walls and floor, I could have laughed with relief to see homely wooden boards and shelves. He lit a lamp that was suspended from a rough-cut beam in the ceiling. I could see now that the windows were heavily shuttered as though to make sure that no streak of light would be seen from the outside. This lighted plot, this wooden cabin, was safety and shelter. Outside was darkness and all manner of unknown terrors.

The way that Jem slipped from one mood into another

was very bewildering; but the important thing was that he *knew*. I did not know and Bowler Hat did not know, either. But Jem did. And I was prepared to listen to him, do what he told me and follow him wherever he might want to lead.

CHAPTER II

FRIENDS OR ENEMIES

I soon discovered that the cabin was reasonably well equipped. Jem pulled some blankets out of a long wooden chest that lay against the wall also serving as a seat and we wrapped ourselves in these while our clothes were drying in front of an oil stove that flickered away and gave out a cheerful warmth. On top there was a saucepan of water to make tea.

Yes, it was a fine cabin. It measured perhaps twenty feet by thirty, with clean boarded floor and three bunks, one over the other at one end, the end farthest away from where we were around the oil stove. There was no decoration in the cabin, nothing in the way of pictures or ornaments and it had all the appearance of having been out of use for some time. I thought, therefore, that there was not much fear of the rightful owners coming back and surprising us, for it did not occur to me that Jem might be the rightful owner of the cabin. Had he not lost his memory like me? What does a man possess when he loses his memory, then? A man who remembers nothing, possesses nothing. But Jem was thoroughly at home. He opened a cupboard and took out a fat, red luncheon sausage, two small loaves, a brown paper bag which we found to contain apples and a cardboard box full of preserved ginger. He made tea by scattering the tea on top of the boiling water and allowing

it to simmer for a while. The tea was very strong and we had to drink it without milk or sugar. But we were in great need of it and the food that Jem had produced. I began to feel very cheerful and snug.

"As soon as I saw you I realised who you were," said Jem. "There's two more of them, I said to myself. Two more that they've done for. I could see by the way you were looking at that signpost, that the same trick had been played on you as had been played on me, aye, and on a good many others as well. I tell you what it is, it's a plot of the very devil himself. There's been nothing like it."

"What is?" asked Bowler Hat, happily munching an apple. I could sense that he did not approve of Jem, had made up his mind to disbelieve everything he said, and was

28

already preparing his own plan of action. This idea made me very angry. The important thing was to give Jem all the support we were capable of, I thought.

" Do you know what they call it when you lose your memory like we have? They call it amnesia, that's the proper word for it. Now it's no such unusual thing to suffer from amnesia as you might think. It happens to dozens of people. But it just doesn't—it just doesn't "—and he emphasised the word by bringing his fist down on to the palm of his hand—" happen quite as often as it has happened to-day. Aye, and yesterday and the day before. Because do you imagine that you are the only people suffering from amnesia in these parts? I tell you that not more than ten minutes' walk from this place there are a dozen of them, all living together, trying to find out just what it is that has caused them to forget. Believe me, this is no ordinary problem. In order to solve it we shall have to use all the wits and courage we have. We are surrounded by enemies. That is the only way of explaining what has happened. There is somebody—some group of people—who are setting out to destroy us all."

Even Bowler Hat had stopped crunching the apple and was listening carefully.

" Listen, I'll tell you what it is, mates." Jem leaned forward and spoke quietly as though the enemy might indeed be listening outside the shutters. " We're on to a big thing. There is not the slightest doubt that somebody is setting out to gain control of this country by black magic. Yes, that's what you can call it, black magic! Think of everybody in the country not knowing who they are, not knowing where they are. Think how blind and helpless they are. Families will be broken up because a father will not know his children, brother will not know sister, everybody will be against everybody else—with the exception of the group of men who are organising this devilish revolution. They will know. And because they will know they will have power. You suspect me, don't you? Oh, I know that you suspect me. It's only natural. You don't know who I am. Well, this will soon be happening all over the country, everybody suspecting everybody else, because they will be robbed of the guiding-line through life, their memories. We've got to find out who this gang is and we've got to stop them. Otherwise, there will be no freedom. We shall be their slaves."

"I'm beginning to remember who I am," said Bowler Hat unexpectedly.

"What?" Jem threw himself back on his heels and shouted in amazement. "You're lying. You don't remember anything. It's a miracle that you can remember the English language, that you can remember how to walk, how to eat. What would you think of yourself if you had to discover all those things for yourself once more? You don't remember, I tell you. You're lying."

I whole-heartedly agreed with what Jem was shouting. He was very angry and I thought he was right to be angry. It was just perverse stubbornness that made Bowler Hat talk like that.

"Yes, I can remember just little things. It'll all come back soon." He went on talking quietly and with great dignity, quite unshaken by Jem's outburst. It was raining again and I could hear the drops pattering on the roof. The wind was moaning. "I remember my fine house, for example. I can see it just as though it is in a dream. Red brick with an avenue of elm trees leading down to the lodge house. Very fine, dignified house. Then there is my servant. I can see his face, gentlemen, small, foxy-faced man but very clean and quick——"

"You liar, you liar, you liar," shouted Jem half-way between rage and laughter. "It's not true. Look at your clothes. Rags and tatters! I'll tell you what you are, my fine gentleman with the red brick house. You're a tramp, a vagabond, an idle good-for-nothing! I know you! Oh, my Lord, a gentleman! Well, this beats everything!"

"How dare you talk to me like this, sir," said Bowler Hat with great dignity. "The moment I can get in touch with the police you will soon see whether I am right or not."

"The police—oh my, just listen to him! Why, you poor fish, how dare you lie to us in this way! This is treachery! You know as well as I do that you remember absolutely nothing of your past. It is quite impossible that you should. Listen to me, I tell you! Don't turn your head away!"

"I think you're a very impertinent young man. There is not much doubt who you are, anyway. An errand boy, I should say."

Jem went quite pink with rage. "And what is wrong with an errand boy? He's a human being, isn't he? You—— In any case, I do not know who I am. All I know is that we are in danger and we are not going to be helped by traitors like you."

"How do you know he is not speaking the truth?" I asked.

"I know he is not speaking the truth, and that is quite good enough." It was true. It was quite good enough for me.

There was quite a fierce quarrel between Jem and the

gentleman who still stuck to his story. "That is how the enemy sometimes works," said Jem eventually. "They give you false memories and you spend your life trying to discover something which does not exist. You're after an illusion, my friend. If I were not here to protect you to-morrow morning, you would be off looking for your red house. It does not exist. And when you don't find it, you go mad. You spend your whole life looking for it, hopeless, but always hoping. Trust me and I will straighten things out."

When I awoke on the following morning, someone was already whistling and clattering about the cabin. Opening my eyes, I was startled to find the ceiling within a foot of my nose. When I rolled over on to my side and looked into the room bright with the morning sunshine that streamed in through the open door and windows, I remembered that I had chosen to pass the night in the topmost bunk. As I looked down and yawned, Jem came in through the door, carrying a tin bowl of water. He saw that I was awake.

"Come on! All's well and a fine morning," he said cheerily. "Dangle your foot over the side and give Bowler Hat a kick in the face."

I would have done no such thing, of course, but in any case, Bowler Hat stuck his tousled head out of the bunk below mine. "A coffin," he said immediately. "Sleeping in a bunk is just like sleeping in a coffin. The dreams it gives you."

As he climbed out of the bunk, Jem placed the bowl of water on the top of the stove. He told us a story about a Chinaman who saved up for years to buy his own coffin so that he could have the pleasure of sleeping in it, only to become so poor eventually that he had to chop it up in order to make a fire that would save him from freezing to death.

I was pleased to see that Bowler Hat and he were now on much better terms. There was nothing very conciliatory about Jem who knew his own mind too definitely to do any climbing down; he had won. It was quite clear that Bowler Hat had had to give way and it was certainly true that we heard nothing more of the red brick house that day.

Jem's story of the night before, telling us of the fiendish plot to gain control of the country by this unheard of and inhuman way of causing people to forget who they were, had naturally made a great impression on me. The only thing that gave me any cause for cheerfulness was Jem himself. He was so bright and keen, his eyes everywhere, his tongue so ready with a cheerful word. I felt that in the coming struggle we had every chance of success. Any quarrelling now between us would be fatal and it was for this particular reason that I was so pleased at what seemed to me to be a reconciliation. I am afraid that I did not have very much respect for Bowler Hat. He was elderly, very respectable, the sort of man who would make a very good mayor or magistrate, I thought. He didn't stir my imagination. Jem did.

I had so much confidence in Jem that it never occurred to me to ask where he got all his supplies and equipment from. Since the enemy had robbed Jem of his memory he had certainly not been inactive. This cabin, for example—and the food he brought out! Everything was so free and easy, and I even began to enjoy the holiday atmosphere, forgetting the danger in which we lay. It was not really cold in the cabin and I had slept with only one rough blanket thrown over me but there was sufficient bite in the morning air to set the blood tingling. It was spring-time.

We gratefully ate the breakfast that Jem had prepared for us. He was of the managing type who takes it for granted that he knows everything, so that in time other people come to take it for granted, too. We had cocoa, bread and luncheon sausage.

We had a little difficulty about washing because apparently Jem expected us to wash in the same small bowl of water. He pointed out that if we were going to rough it, and we were, we might as well begin at once. Bowler Hat had been rather silent since getting up but he reached the bowl before I did and when my turn came the water was dirty. I could not bring myself to wash in it and said so. Jem had a scowl on his face. " I had to walk a mile and a half to get a bucket of water and we don't waste it in washing. It'll be your turn to wash first to-morrow. That fair? "

I washed.

The three of us went outside and stood in the morning sun.

" Well, young gentlemen," said Bowler Hat, cheerfully taking out his whistle, " I think we had better be starting."

" Where for? " asked Jem suddenly.

Bowler Hat began trilling on his whistle. His fingers were plump but nimble and although he could never manage to play a proper tune, nevertheless he was able to run gaily up and down a scale. His bowler hat was perched on the back of his head.

" Eh? " He broke off short. " Well, I should think there's a town of some sort close to here. We'd best be off and put ourselves into the hands of the doctor."

" What doctor? " said Jem, drawing closer to him.

" When a man loses his memory, the best thing he can do is to go to the doctor. That's what we ought to do.

34

Then the police, so as they can find out who we are. I don't like not knowing who I am." I thought, with dismay, that the quarrel was going to begin all over again. I had been much too optimistic. But this time Jem did not lose his temper.

"What you say is impossible. And if you like I'll tell you why it's impossible. But let's go for our morning walk first."

He began leading the way over the top of the hill and such was the force of example that Bowler Hat and I found ourselves following. But Bowler Hat was grumbling. "At least I want to know where I am. That's a reasonable enough sort of request. How does a man recover his memory? Well, he sees things he's seen before and they remind him."

At the back of the cabin was a small field that had been freshly ploughed and Jem began picking his way across it. He turned back and said, "That's not how the Enemy goes to work. They see to it that when they rob a man of his memory, they set him down in another part of the country. There's no danger of him remembering. What's more, they make it as difficult as possible for him—they put him in a part of the country where the people are hostile to him."

"How can that be? How can people be hostile to us?" I asked. But Jem did not answer and I rather had the impression there was a very simple answer to my question which I should have been able to see for myself. Bowler Hat did not seem to be listening now. He was playing on his whistle.

Large white birds were sweeping over the new ploughed land and squealing like cats. Then we climbed over a stile and Jem kept plucking grasses and flowers and telling us their names. And then at the very top of the next rise there

was another stile and as we approached it we could look between its wooden bars at the blue sky, for it might have stood on the edge of a cliff. Bowler Hat had pushed on a little in front, whistling as he went but when he came to the stile he stopped, his head turning from side to side.

"We can have our conference here," said Jem.

I had picked a few blue flowers and came last. The screaming white birds swept above our heads as the three of us gazed at the sudden, startling spectacle of the ocean itself, taking up threequarters of the horizon and coming gently up to the golden fringe of sand, no more than a mile from where we were standing. The sea was the clear, stainless blue of the flowers that I held in my hand, its glassy surface untroubled by any boat.

"Reminds me of something," said Bowler Hat.

We settled ourselves on the stile and began our debate.

"The first thing we've got to get into our heads is this," said Jem. "I've lost my memory longer than you chaps and therefore I know more. I've had to learn from bitter experience. What I've learned is that the police are the very people we've got to watch out for."

"These are very revolutionary thoughts, young man. I have always regarded the policeman as the very defender——"

Jem interrupted him quite rudely. "Your memory was never so bad as it is now. This is the thing. The police of this particular district are dangerous."

"Why?" I asked, looking out to sea.

"Listen! Up to not so very long ago, this part of the country was like the Garden of Eden. This is what I'm told. I've had to spy the land out. I don't quite know why it was, but everybody was law-abiding. No thieving. No crime. The jails were empty. No sooner did the magistrate get into his court than he went home again. Nobody to try. The police spent most of their time just wearing out shoe leather and noting down cases of swine fever, until it got so bad at last that the cops used to hide in the hedges of a night, to catch fellows riding push-bikes without a light. But everyone had proper lamps so they couldn't find work that way. At last, things got to such a pitch that folk began to say that the police-force was an extravagant waste of money if there were no criminals. And the best thing would be to do away with the police-force altogether."

"It sounds a very reasonable idea," said Bowler Hat, interested, in spite of himself.

Jem lowered his voice and looked round. "Now I'm not quite sure about what I'm going to say. But I've been putting two and two together and making five of them. And this is what I think. The police got scared that they would lose their jobs. They got scared when people marched round the streets shouting, ' Do away with the police and lower the rates' and ' Kick out the constables'. ' Give us free electric light instead'."

This was an extraordinary state of affairs, I thought. I had never heard of anything like this in my life before.

" The police got so scared that there was an immediate crime wave. Houses got robbed, people were held up and threatened with murder. In other words—because there were no house-breakers and thieves, the police arranged for a few robberies to happen just to make sure that their jobs would not be taken away from them."

" I don't believe a word of it. It is quite fantastic. It is against the law." Bowler Hat was quite indignant about it. " This is just the sort of thing that should be disclosed by a very strong letter to *The Times*. But it's not true."

" What do you mean ' It's not true '? " cried Jem, springing off the stile and confronting us. " You say it is not true because you are afraid of the truth. I *know*. You don't know. During the past few months think how I've sweated and toiled to get my bits and pieces of information together! Think how I've had to organise! And then you calmly sit there saying that it's not true. Remember this "—he was beside himself with rage—" when I came to, after losing my memory, there was nobody to give me a helping hand. Nobody. No cabin, no trousers, no cocoa——"

" I'm sure I'm very much obliged——"

"And think of the terror of being alone, not knowing, not daring to think. I was the forerunner, I was the person who prepared for all the others—I tell you there are a dozen of us in a cave under those cliffs "—he flung out one arm and I looked at the cool, green curve of the cliff—" preparing for the battle against the enemy. All with blank, empty minds. Then you question me! You say it is lies—— ! "

" I'm sure I'm very much obliged," repeated Bowler Hat calmly, " but I should like you to remember, young man, that I am at least twice your age and I must ask you for a little more respect." He gave a little trill on his pipe. Jem looked at him speechless. "And there's one other thing I should like to ask you, young man. If you're so sure that these strange people exist who want to—ah—— ! " I could see that he had a disgust of even uttering the idea.

" Who want to rule the country by the weapon of amnesia," said Jem with vehemence.

" In short, who are they? "

" In short," said Jem, as though he had come to a great decision. " They are the police! "

Bowler Hat came down from the stile. He looked at Jem unbelievingly. " This is a very disgraceful state of affairs. What does the Chief Constable say about it? "

" That's the man," said Jem. " The Chief Constable."

" I shall go and see him myself," said Bowler Hat, putting his whistle into his pocket. " I have never heard anything so disgraceful in my life. What a way to reward the tax-payers, indeed. I shall certainly have to show him what's what."

" You forget," said Jem with a superior smile, " that the moment you set foot in the town you will be arrested. The police are on the look out for you. They know you. They count on you as one of their victims."

" Then—— " said Bowler Hat, his whole world whirling about his ears.

"Then, the only thing to do is to believe me when I tell you things. Even if you are twice my age, give me a bit of confidence. Not done so bad so far, have we? Well, we'll keep on like this. The only way to corner these fellows is with craft, craft. And who's got craft?" Jem tapped himself on the chest. "Me."

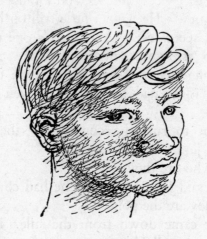

CHAPTER III

THE BOXING BOOTH

NEVERTHELESS, now began one of the periods of Not-Knowing. I think my confidence in Jem was a little shaken when he said that we must do something about money, that we couldn't live on air, and where did we think the apples and luncheon sausage came from?

"Ah! That's what I should like to know, young man," said Bowler Hat. But he was not so critical of Jem as he had been. He seemed to have settled down to what one could almost call an enjoyment of having lost his memory. It was true in a way. Not knowing who you were took a great deal of responsibility off your shoulders.

But I was anxious to go to the cave where Jem said the other members of the party, our allies against the enemy, were to be found. Jem was much taken up by the problem of obtaining money. At length he came to a decision.

"There's a smallish town not five miles from here. There's nothing for it. We'll have to go and see what we can pick up."

"And the police?" I asked.

"We shall have to disguise ourselves."

"Impossible," said Bowler Hat. "I refuse to disguise myself."

I was enthusiastic. Jem himself was disappointed to find that a false moustache was out of the question. It was easy enough to pick up a piece of wool rubbed off a sheep's back but there was no gum to stick it on with. "The best thing," said Jem, "is to disguise ourselves as gipsies, which could be done by rubbing earth on our hands and faces to darken them."

"I regard the whole idea as absurd," repeated Bowler Hat and began muttering about a red-brick house standing in fine park land once more. But he realised, of course, that Jem and he were agreed in one point, the necessity of getting to a town and I had a suspicion that he there planned to desert us. In any case, I thought it strange that he should now quietly submit to having his hands and face stained with earth. Jem wanted to cut off his moustache but he gave such a hoot of alarm at the very idea that it was obviously useless to persist in the idea.

And it would be dark when we got to the town. That was another thing in our favour. I think Jem was disappointed with the effectiveness of our disguises but apparently the need of money was so great that we were justified in taking a few risks.

By the time we had made all our preparations it was afternoon. We drank some more tea, finished off the luncheon sausage, locked the box-tricycle in the cabin and set off on our journey, Bowler Hat pulling his whistle out of his pocket now and again as though not knowing whether to play or not and then deciding against a performance as that would rob him of some very necessary breath needed for the journey.

"I am quite prepared, as a great concession," he remarked as we were passing the signpost with the arms pointing to

Yes and No, "to allow you to call me Mr. Bowler." He was very insistent on the Mr. part of it. Jem glanced at me. We said nothing.

I was still puzzled about that signpost. I had asked Jem what it could possibly signify but his answer had neither informed me nor encouraged me to repeat my inquiry. Eventually, I decided that the police, in organising their crime wave, had decided to deface the signpost by obliterating the correct names and then, at last, as a sort of joke, writing the words Yes and No in red ink. I knew that it was a criminal offence to deface a signpost.

The road went up and down like a switchback and we had made perhaps three ascents and three descents when we came in sight of the place we were making for, the small town. We had been walking away from the sea for perhaps an hour and a half and the sky was already beginning to darken. The red houses of the market town seemed gathered round the fine spire of the church but what particularly caught the eye were the many fruit orchards in blossom. They were so thick round the town that the church and houses might have been floating on a fine-spun foam, white, white, white, but flecked with pink and green. But Jem was not interested in the fruit blossom.

"There," he pointed, "there's where we're going to make a packet of money if we keep our eyes about us." And he pointed. I saw then that to the north of the little town, a number of tents had been pitched and even at this distance we could faintly hear the sound of a fair-organ. It was, most certainly, a fair. A finger of grey smoke was going up from among the tents, probably from a caravan fire.

"Things will be pretty well under way by the time we get there, young 'un."

"I feel exhausted and must rest," remarked Mr. Bowler mildly. "I trust that we are going to make the money in a perfectly honest way."

"What do you take me for," demanded Jem. "'Course it'll be honest. Can you imagine me doing anything dishonest?"

"Yes, I'm afraid I can."

Jem ignored the remark. "We'll skirt the town and make our way straight to the fair ground."

By the time we had reached the edge of the fruit orchards (the distance was very deceptive and much farther than it had looked) it was already dark, but the moon had risen early. The sky overhead was finely scattered with stars and through the branches of the trees we could see the lights of the town. But in front of us was a greater glare, a confusion of coloured lights and a slowly rising mushroom of golden smoke.

"Remember," said Jem, "if you see a cop, don't bat an eyelid. Keep your head."

We walked on silently.

"Keep out of trouble, whatever we do," he said quietly. "But be on the look out for it always. If there *is* any trouble—well, just watch the police! Wouldn't surprise me if they weren't organising a wholesale robbery of the takings."

We went in through the gate of the field where the fair was now in full swing. Although I had thought the sound of the music and the brilliance of the lights would have exhilarated me, for some reason I was oppressed by the feeling of Not-Knowing. Perhaps it was the thought that we were without money and with no very clear way of obtaining any. We were in the middle of a happy crowd of country people, all determined to enjoy themselves and it occurred to me that if you have no money, never go and watch other people spend theirs. If you have no friends, never watch a gang of happy people enjoying themselves. Yes, it was one of the wretched Not-Knowing feelings and I was suddenly tempted to turn tail, run out of the fairground, desert Jem and Mr. Bowler, find one of the policemen and try to explain just what had happened. What Jem had said about the police was just too inconceivable. I felt in the need of comfort and certitude. I suspected that Mr. Bowler felt much the same.

We were standing just outside a group that had gathered round a strong man who was lifting hundredweight bars as easily as you like. Then he allowed two assistants to loop a rope around his neck. It was a long rope, about twelve feet, and the assistants, taking hold of the two ends, stood as far away as its length would permit them. The strong man folded his arms and looked round with such a pleased expression on his face that he might have been going to have his photograph taken. But suddenly, as though on a signal, the two assistants leaned on the rope and pulled with all their strength. They put all their weight behind it. The rope was still looped round the strong man's neck. He was holding his breath and his face went quite red. It must have been an immense strain. And then I could see that his nostrils were beginning to quiver and knew that he had had enough. The two assistants dropped the rope, the strong man took a step forward and bowed; and there was a burst of handclapping and a few pennies were tossed on to a strip of canvas at his feet. The assistants went round with the cap, so we went away.

" That's given me an idea," said Jem. " If that fellow can earn money so easily, so can we."

45

"I'm not going to be strangled for anybody, if that's what you mean," said Mr. Bowler rather quickly, for Jem was looking at him.

"No, not that sort of thing, Mr. Samson. Now what do you think of this; you can be my two assistants and I'll do the performing."

"Performing of what?"

"My imitations. Look, what do you think this is?" He had led the way round behind a coconut booth. He took up a prancing sort of attitude with his posterior stuck grotesquely out, his left hand resting on it and the arm crooked. The right hand he held up to his forehead, the back of the wrist resting against his brow, the fingers stiff and pointing straight forward like a beak or a spout. "There. What's that?"

"A hen," I suggested rather tentatively.

"Some sort of bird," murmured Mr. Bowler, anxious not to give offence.

"Hen, bird, no! It's a teapot. Can't you tell? Then what about this?" He held his right arm out stiffly before him, his left arm pointing behind. He stood solemnly on one leg and allowed the other to swing rhythmically backwards and forwards. "What's that?"

Neither Mr. Bowler nor I had the faintest idea.

"It's a grandfather clock, see?"

For some reason or other, these imitations made Mr. Bowler so indignant that he could hardly speak. I think he thought that Jem was trying to pull his leg but I knew that Jem was honestly trying to think of some way of obtaining money quickly. Even so, I had to smile. I had almost forgot my feeling of Not-Knowing.

"No, it's not a bit of use," said Mr. Bowler bluntly.

46

"You'd only make a fool of yourself. There, young man, and you know my opinion and no mistake."

"Oh, really!" Jem was in a heat. "Then let's see if you've got any ideas about getting rich quick."

Mr. Bowler was of much too even a temperament to be stung by any taunt like this and looked round the fairground with the air of a general surveying a battlefield. "Well, what about that over there, then?"

He waved our attention over to a large booth standing next to the great roundabout. It was a boxing booth and standing on the platform outside was the owner, promoter, or whatever it is you call him. He was addressing the crowd and banging on a drum. By his side stood an enormous negro dressed only in a pair of crimson shorts. His black body glistened as though he had wiped himself down with oil; the thousand lights of the fairground played on his gleaming body. He was beautifully made but for all that he seemed a very miserable negro. His arms were folded and he was motionless. He looked down at the boards at his feet, not glaring round at the crowd as one might have expected a prize fighter to do. We were too far away to hear what the promoter was shouting but there was a notice behind him large enough for anyone to read. It was to this that Mr. Bowler had pointed, and I realised now that he did so as a means of pulling Jem's leg. "Five pounds to any man who lasts a round with Jack White. £50 to any man who knocks him out." Mr. Bowler certainly did not expect Jem to take on the negro. Undoubtedly the negro was the Jack White referred to and, as I said, he looked a very miserable black man.

So Jem's next action surprised us. He stooped and picked up a piece of coloured paper, the remnants of a comic hat that the wind was moving uneasily over the grass. Carefully

flattening it out over his knee, he then proceeded to tear it into strips about an inch wide. He trimmed them off so that one was about nine inches long, another was six inches and the last a mere three.

"We're going to draw lots," he said when he had gathered the papers up into his fist so that the ends, all level, alone were showing.

"No, not me," said Mr. Bowler immediately. "If there's no other way of getting money than by fighting Mr. White, then I'm ready to starve. I've a better idea. I can play on my whistle and you can dance." I felt that neither Jem nor Mr. Bowler were taking the draw very seriously.

Now it was the turn for Jem to be really magnificent. Yes, in that moment he became truly heroic, put an end to my mood of Not-Knowing and, in my imagination, donned shining armour, mounted on a champing steed and sallied forth to challenge the world. He laughed and tossed the coloured papers on to the grass. The sound of the fair was all around us. For the first time, I noticed that a girl was sitting on the steps of a caravan, peeling potatoes. She put her knife down and looked at us. "There's only one thing to be done, then," said Jem. "I'll have to take the job on myself. As for you," he went on, turning to me, "it's not to be expected that you could take on a fellow like Jack White but I did expect some other people, with a bit more weight, to back me up." He was very bitter.

"Young man," said Mr. Bowler, "I have been very patient with you. More out of a spirit of generosity than anything else I have borne with you. And I have been curious to see what you propose doing. You're a young man of character—bad character, no doubt, but it's quite possible to get to like you. In order to please you I would have done anything within reason but to go into the ring with that negro is certainly not reason. There!" Undoubtedly, Mr. Bowler thought that he had made a very generous speech.

Jem did not even bother to answer but started to walk away. I caught him by the sleeve and asked him where he was going. "To fight the blackie, of course," he replied, "since there's no-one else. All right now, all right now." I think he was a little embarrassed by my evident admiration. "Come into the booth or stay out, I don't mind. Meet me after the show if you want your share of the fifty quid."

Mr. Bowler planted himself in Jem's way. "Now, young man, from your own point of view I must ask you to reconsider——"

Jem gently pushed him aside.

"—because you're not much more than a lad yourself."

"Come and watch me then."

We went. And if you don't think much of Mr. Bowler and me for letting Jem take on the fight, then you have never seen a shining negro like Jack White nor known a determined fanatic like Jem.

Our discussion behind the booth had not taken more than five minutes, so when we reached the boxing booth the crowd had barely begun to go in. Jack White had disappeared but the promoter with his drum was still there looking down with some satisfaction on the steady stream of silver that was passing over the pay-box counter.

Immediately I took Jem by the arm. "You can't do it."

"Why not?"

"We haven't any money." I was surprised to find how relieved I was to think that Jem could not undertake the fight after all. "You won't get in."

"Oh, who won't?" Jem snorted and marched straight up to the promoter. "Hey, mister!" he shouted up. At first the man did not hear him and Jem had to bang on the boards with the heel of his hand to attract attention.

"Eh?" he grunted. "Well, what d'you want? Come on now. Cough it up. I can't stand 'ere all night." All this came out in one breath, and Jem, although he had his mouth open to pop a word in, had to wait until the man had finished.

"I'll fight your nigger," he said.

"You'll what?" The promoter put his drum to one side and looked down at Jem. Then he threw back his head and opened his mouth so that I could see one yellow tooth shining in the top gum. At first he laughed very faintly, gasping for breath and then, when he was able to bring his face down, he bellowed with the kind of he-ho-ing laughter that giants in fairy stories are supposed to be expert in. In the middle of his laughter he took hold of himself and frowned like a magistrate. " Go away. Go away with you," he said, as though we were birds on his bean patch.

" I said I'd fight your nigger," Jem shouted. By now, quite a number of people had gathered round to hear what was going on. The boxing promoter looked round and did a bit of quick thinking.

" Go on, boss," shouted somebody in the crowd. " Let 'em in! 'Fraid he'll bash the nigger."

"A respectable-looking man like you," said the promoter to Mr. Bowler, who looked indignant.

" We've got no money," said Jem. He had the crowd on his side and the man on the platform had to alter his tactics. " I only wanted to save your life," he said. " Jackie will eat you. All right, pass in there."

" And my friends," insisted Jem.

" 'Ow many are there? Those two. All right, pass in there. Don't blame me. I warned you. Ought to be ashamed of yourself," he added to Mr. Bowler. We passed in.

It was very hot and steamy inside the booth although there were probably not more than seventy or eighty spectators packed round the ring; the smallness of the booth gave me the impression that the entire population of the town were present. There was a roped-off narrow approach to the ring itself and the three of us managed to work our way round to the part of the ring where the boxers would have to climb over a rope. I could still hear the banging of the drum outside. I looked at Jem and saw that there was a strange half-smile on his face and he kept opening and closing his hands as though in anticipation. He was excited but he was suppressing it. There was not a trace of apprehension in his bearing. He looked eagerly around the booth and turning whispered something to me which I did not catch. Mr. Bowler cleared his throat noisily and glowered about fiercely.

Here and there a man began to whistle shrilly. The crowd was beginning to get impatient. The yellow light of the arc lamp over the ring was swirling with tobacco smoke. Someone threw a small object, an orange or something like that, from one side of the booth to the other. For the moment, I thought it was a bird.

The really interesting bouts were kept back and for the first quarter of an hour we had to watch youths, not more than seventeen or eighteen, boxing each other fiercely around the ring. There was a great deal of ducking and weaving and even I, inexperienced as I was, could see that this was not the real thing. The fighters were not setting out to hurt one another and the crowd was quickly on to this, booing and jeering until the end of the round. I suppose the proprietor must have said something to the young pugilists then for, from the stroke of the gong in the next round, they were pummelling into each other so that even the bloodthirstiest of the spectators had nothing to grumble about.

Now and again I could hear Jem laughing to himself and see his shoulders shaking. Mr. Bowler looked over at me inquiringly but I could only shrug my shoulders and shake my head.

Jack White jumped under the rope and gave an exhibition

of shadow boxing. For such a heavy man, he must have been over fourteen stone, he glided round the ring like a ballet dancer. Then as the applause died down, came the moment we were all waiting for. The promoter was in the middle of the ring holding his right arm in the air and calling for silence.

"To-night, ladies and gentlemen, we are especially lucky. Jack White on my right 'ere 'as a challenger." There was a burst of cheering at this. "And you know what that means. Fifty pounds if 'e knocks Jackie out and five pounds if 'e lasts a round. Now mister, where are you?" There was a broad grin on the promoter's face.

"Here I am," said Jem calmly and climbed into the ring. He nodded down to Mr. Bowler and myself, then walked over to the centre of the ring. Jack White did not even raise his head as his challenger came up. Such a show of confidence and contempt rather alarmed me. I could only imagine that it was Jem's plan to keep out of the negro's way for at least one round. He was probably quicker on his feet, being smaller and very nippy, than Jack White.

"We'll give you time to change," the promoter called over.

"I'll do like this." Jem took his hands out of his pocket. As soon as he had turned his back to walk to his corner, Jack White looked up slowly and clapped his gloved hands together. Some of the crowd had begun to jeer as soon as they had seen Jem's slight build, but his truly astonishing calmness mystified them and they fell silent in expectation. Even I began to think that he had something up his sleeve and felt more cheerful. But the negro's face remained quite without expression. He took in Jem with his slow glance but there was nothing on his broad, flat features to show that he despised or respected his opponent.

53

Jem tied up one of his shoes and the gong went. The gloves had been expertly whipped on by one of the seconds. He was in the centre of the ring immediately, waiting for the negro who came out of his corner slowly. There was an almost terrifying silence in the booth. Then Jem flicked out his left fist and caught White on the forearm. He danced away again before the negro could follow up. Yes, there was not much doubt about it. Jem was relying on speed to keep out of the way of White until the gong went.

White was always trying to work Jem into a corner but he had a wily opponent and at times Jem doubled up like a pocket-knife at the ropes and dodged under the negro's arms out of what might have been a dangerous position. The crowd, of course, enjoyed all this immensely. Jem's chances of knocking the negro out were, to say the least of it, remote and this trick of playing for time delighted them. They began to boo White. He shook his head and bored in again.

Then, for the first time, I began to get suspicious of White. Jem was nippy, certainly, but so was White as he had shown in his display of shadow boxing. Now, in this fight with Jem he seemed ridiculously slow. Jem could land a punch on the negro's chest and dance away out of reach like lightning. I felt sure that White was not putting everything into the fight. For some reason or other he was resisting the temptation to knock Jem out of the ring as he might easily have done. I looked over to where the promoter was standing and what I saw there confirmed my suspicions. The man's face was struggling between expressions of bewilderment and rage. There was little doubt that White's other challengers had been put safely out of the ring by this time.

The crowd began to cheer as soon as the gong sounded to tell us that Jem had won five pounds. Five pounds! Mr. Bowler and I struggled over to Jem's corner and I made ready to help him down.

"Down? I'm going on. Five pounds a round, you know." I had forgotten that the fight was not over yet. Jem would say nothing about the negro's strange tactics. Mr. Bowler knew no more about boxing than I did but he was ready to give Jem advice. "In my considered opinion, the best thing to do is to keep swinging your arms about."

In Jack White's corner a great deal of discussion was going on. The promoter was standing with his legs apart, wagging his head fiercely and holding his clenched fist in the air. The negro sat on his stool quite motionless, looking down at the ground. It occurred to me that he might be ill.

The gong went for the start of the second round and then an astonishing thing happened. I had barely time to step away from the ringside when Jem had danced out into the centre of the ring and punched White in the solar plexus. A hooter on one of the roundabouts wailed and White fell forward on his face like so much wood. Talk about David and Goliath! The crowd yelled its approval as though each one of them had won the fifty pounds. Jem remained standing in the ring looking at the boxing promoter as he knelt over the prostrate pugilist.

On the promoter's face, when he straightened his back and held up his hand for silence, there was a look that could almost be called defiant. "White was ill," he announced. "He wasn't fit to fight. Under those circumstances, I'm calling the fight off. Mind you, I . . ."

But the rest of his announcement was drowned by the

sudden clamour of the crowd. They were all shouting that Jem should receive the fifty pounds and men in the back row pressed threateningly forward towards the ring. The promoter's lips were moving but I could hear no words. He was trying to get the next contest going, so that even while Jack White was being dragged from the ring, two young men in orange shorts were boxing away in one corner. But it was no good! The crowd was going to have none of this. "We want fifty pounds! We want fifty smackers!" Booing for White and cheering for Jem in turn. Caps, pieces of paper, every odd piece of rubbish that came to hand, were thrown into the ring and then they began to pull the place down. There was a sound of splintering wood as the benches at the back were torn up; someone with a knife had slit one of the canvas walls and a gust of cool night air came in. Pieces of wood were thrown at the light. There was always the danger of fire and my thoughts were mainly about getting out safely. Like a man demented, the promoter was standing in the ring holding up a bundle of notes and shouting. But now they were in the mood the men were going to wreck the place and a couple of hundred pounds would not have deterred them.

Jack White was sitting up in a corner and I had just time to see Jem bending over him when the crowd began clambering into the ring and he was hidden from view. I made a move in his direction for by now I suppose that the sudden turn events had taken had bewildered and excited me. I may even have thought that Jem was in danger, which was ridiculous. But no sooner had I made a step when a heavy hand grasped me by the shoulder.

"Out, my young friend, and as quickly as we can go. That is the course indicated, I think." It was Mr. Bowler, pushing me through the crowd, using me as a sort of battering ram to force a passage. He had such a tight hold upon me that I was helpless. This so enraged me that I believe I would have hacked his shins. But at that moment we heard the shrilling of police whistles and Mr. Bowler jerked me away from the exit, up over the wooden seats and then, when we had reached the back of the booth said, " Now, each for himself and the devil take the hindermost." He had found a slit in the canvas and pitched me through, head first.

I fell awkwardly on my shoulder on a pile of sacking but with my head well tucked in. I sat in the long grass and rubbed myself. For one moment Mr. Bowler flapped like a great bat above me, grunted and then dropped on to the sacking. We were on the side of the booth away from the fair. There were excited shouts as people hurried over to see what all the trouble was about. Someone was blowing a police whistle inside the boxing booth itself. We had played straight into their hands and no mistake. There had been no crimes or disturbances to keep the police occupied, Jem had said, but as soon as we appear on the scene, a minor civil war breaks out. It would be enough to make any police sergeant rub his hands.

I knew what Mr. Bowler intended doing. His plan was to creep out of the fairground while the creeping was good.

" We must wait for Jem," I whispered.

" Come on, now," he said, shaking his head so violently that his hat fell off.

" I'm going to wait," I said in my most determined way. I spoke more loudly now. Mr. Bowler's next act took me quite by surprise. He caught me round the waist and slung me over his left shoulder like a wounded soldier. I pounded him in the back with my fists but he set his bowler straight with his right hand and stumbled off behind the caravans. He was making off towards the darkness of that part of the meadow where the fair had not extended itself. He suddenly stopped and I could hear him breathing hard.

" Well, it's all over now and no mistake," he said.

For the first time I noticed that the shouting from the boxing booth could no longer be heard, although the rest of the fair, the pipe organs in particular, was still raising a cheerful din.

" You can put me down," I said after a while. " You needn't be scared. I shan't run back. Though I must say you're a fine one."

" They've got them now. They arrest anybody and everybody." Mr. Bowler said this with an undisguised note of satisfaction in his voice. " Our brave friend, Jem, will undoubtedly be languishing in the town gaol where we, as his friends and accomplices, might likewise be if it wasn't for my caution and foresight."

" That's just two other words for cowardice," I said.

" Caution and foresight are very valuable qualities in a man. Hallo, what's this here? "

Two figures were running towards us. The illumination of the fairground was behind them and we could see them outlined against it. The chances were, that they could not see us at all, for we were standing in the obscurity.

" Why—it's . . . "

They pounded closer, running side by side. There was not the slightest doubt now. " Jem," I called out. " Thank heavens you got away."

" Hallo, it's you, is it," said Jem, as casually as though he had met us on an afternoon walk. "Allow me to introduce a friend of mine." He turned to the figure with him.

59

" These are a couple of mates of mine, Mr. Bowler and a lad we'll call Roger for the time being."

" It's Jack White," I cried.

" Yes, sir, at your service," said the big negro stepping over. His voice was low and rich but he spoke English with nothing of that comic accent I had half expected. Indeed, he spoke better English than I did.

" Let's get, quick," said Jem. He climbed over a stile and we all followed him.

CHAPTER IV

THE MYSTERY OF THE CAVE

THE MOON was well up by now and there was a delicious perfume coming over from the crowded blossom of the fruit orchards. But we were much too intent on getting away from the town as quickly as possible to have much time for admiring the beauty of the night; the road stretched in front of us, glistening like a snake.

"I am a miserable man, gentlemen," said Jack White when we had put a respectable distance between us and the town. I thought he had every excuse for saying so. It was by no means warm and he had only a long red dressing-gown thrown over his boxing shorts. But I knew that he was not complaining about the cold. "Perhaps the most miserable man that's lived since Job."

Jem was in an excellent mood. He seemed to be vibrating with energy in contrast with the negro, who was plodding along as though he bore all the troubles of the world on his shoulders.

"Surely," said Mr. Bowler, "you have a terrible profession. A life of violence."

To my surprise this stimulated Jack White out of the silence into which he had fallen. "That's just it, sir, and it's not surprising to me that you've hit on it straight away."

So as we walked along in the moonlight, making for I was not at all sure where but hoping that it was for the cabin and some more luncheon sausage, Jack White told us as much of the story of his life as was necessary to explain why Jem had succeeded in knocking him out and why he was here at our side at all.

"I'm a big man and strong. I could break a man's neck with a blow and not much doubt about it. But my nature is peaceable. I am a divided man, divided against myself and that is the cause of my discontent. It seems that I was made to be a fighter and nothing else. I've no brains to talk of, that's quite clear to me now. So the very thing that I can do, I hate. I hate fighting and pain. That is what I think."

I thought Jem was going to interrupt with some remark or other, for what Jack White was saying was surprising enough in itself; and I felt that it was directly opposed to what Jem himself felt about life. I could hear Mr. Bowler making grunts of approval. I was also beginning to feel very hungry.

"Up to about eighteen months ago I didn't have such a bad time," the boxer went on. "Maybe it was two years ago. I was a farmer. That's to say, I worked on a farm, looking after the chickens mostly. You must understand that I was a good sort of a chap. I suppose it was my fault though that I got into a bit of trouble. And I'm not telling you what that trouble was, no sirs. All I'm saying is that I needed some money quick. I'd got no money, not a ha'penny. I didn't know what to do about it. Then it seemed to me that I had one big piece of luck. A travelling fair came to the town, plenty going on, too. I didn't think too much of fairs mind, and don't now. But, as I was just telling you, I wanted cash and there was a chappie at the fair willing to pay five pounds to anyone who would stay in the ring for a round with one of his boxers. It was the same as you saw. Well, you can guess I had a close look at the proposition. I measured myself up in my mind's eye against the fellow that the chappie was putting up and found myself a good bit bigger. So, ready enough now, I got under the ropes. I got the other fellow in the first round—put him through the ropes. It was a fair fight."

At the very memory of the fight, Jack White seemed to grow more cheerful. It was evident that there was something in boxing that attracted him enormously in spite of his theories about its unpleasantness. He had called himself a divided man, meaning that he had the makings of a boxer but none of the disposition. It would probably be truer to say that he had a great liking for boxing tucked away inside him, but there were moments, as now, when his reason told him that he should dislike it.

"And that was that, sirs. They paid me the money straight over and then Gaskin, that's the promoter, took me aside and gave me a talking to.

" 'You're a great boxer,' he said. 'Where d'you learn it, son?'

" 'I'm not a boxer, sir,' I said. 'I'm a chicken farmer.'

" 'Tell you what. I'll give you ten pounds a week to travel round with my show as a boxer. Ten pounds! Now what is it to be?'

" Gaskin persuaded me no end. I didn't like it even then, I can tell you. It was easy money, Gaskin said.

" 'Sure,' I said back, for I was getting twenty-five shillings on the farm. 'Try it for a month, son,' he said, 'and if you don't like it, you can go back.' So that sort of made my mind up. I had to sign a bit of paper which I didn't read and then I set to. It was easy. The young chaps didn't know much about using their fists and I could put them out with my left hand. But I didn't like it. As I told you, I'm a peaceable man and hated wringing a chicken's neck. It was a rotten life. Just imagine it, sirs, doing nothing but punching heads of poor, harmless chaps. If I didn't punch them hard, Gaskin would go wild. By the end of the month he still hadn't paid me. I said I would go.

" ' No you don't, son. I've got this,' he said after a bit and showed me the paper that I had signed.

" ' What's that, boss? ' I said back to him.

" ' This says that you've got to stay with me for five years. It's a contract and you signed it.'

" Of course, the old rogue had tricked me. I'd not read the paper and you can guess how wild I was. He threatened me with all sorts, gaol and whatnot if I tried to get away. What with the other bit of trouble I'd got myself into, I thought I'd best lie low for a bit. He said the contract gave him the right to make me stay. You see why I was miserable? I hated it all. I didn't even like the red boxing shorts they gave me. I wanted to get back to my chickens. And no way as far as I could think of. So, eventually, I got to thinking the only way to go to work would be to pretend to be unable to fight. Because you mustn't think," he said turning to Jem, " that you won that scrap on your own. You mustn't think that I wasn't helping you just a little. And then, when I saw all the trouble that the crowd was making, I had the idea of making a bolt for it."

" No, it was my idea," said Jem suddenly.

" Yes, and that was strange," said the negro thoughtfully. " You did say that but it was in my mind before you spoke."

" Oh, I just guessed that there was something the matter. Quite a valuable addition to our forces, don't you think," he said to Mr. Bowler and me. " Don't you worry," he told Jack White, " everything is in hand now. There's some very important work that you can give us a hand with. But more of that later on. The important thing now is to get to the seashore."

"A lot of nonsense, if you ask me," said Mr. Bowler, for he was in one of his grumbling moods.

As soon as Jem mentioned the sea, I felt cheerful. I remembered how impressed I had been to look at it that very morning and it occurred to me that, before losing my memory, I might have lived on the coast or been otherwise connected with the sea in some way.

"For preference, I should like to go back to the cabin. Though it's a long way," said Mr. Bowler. "All this walking and fighting and excitement. However, Mr. White, I understand your point of view perfectly. I can see that you are a man of peace. The main thing is to get you under cover as quickly as possible or you'll be catching pneumonia, dressed as you are."

"That's just what we're trying to do," said Jem. "Come on."

We now found ourselves standing on a crossroads with no signpost to give us any guide. On the far side of the crossroads was a stunted oak, not a leaf stirring in the windless air. The moonlight was so bright that we could have seen a pin on the road, so it will be understood that there was no difficulty in reading a notice pinned up on the trunk of the tree.

REWARD

FOR INFORMATION LEADING TO THE APPREHENSION OF THE THIEVES WHO UNLAWFULLY TOOK FROM THE FARM OF MR. WILL TWO COWS, FOUR GOATS, AN ASS AND TWO DOZEN EGGS. ALL SUSPICIOUS CHARACTERS TO BE REPORTED TO THE POLICE.

Signed: FELIX DUFF,
Chief of Police.

"Stuff and nonsense," snapped Jem. "I don't believe anybody could steal two cows, four goats, an ass, and two dozen eggs. This is a fake notice put up by the police to keep people on edge. Bah! They're cunning." He reached up and tore the notice down and, telling us to follow him, climbed over a stile and led the way across a dark field towards a swelling hill.

And then a blind man would have known that he was walking by the sea. He would have known it by the salty freshness in the air. There was only the smallest murmur coming out of the night. Yes, there was no doubt about it. To me the sea was an old friend and I stared at it, when suddenly we had come to the top of the hill, as though my past would flash upon its toiling face as on a screen. The last time we had seen the sea had been the morning; but now at night time, with enough light from the moon to cover it with silver, I was even more fascinated. It lay there like a great shield, pitted and worn in battle.

We scrambled down the cliff path, so steep that we had to go down backwards, scrabbling at the earth with our hands to prevent ourselves from falling. Seeing Mr. Bowler in front of me like a great black spider carefully backing away from me, I found it difficult to prevent myself from laughing; it was one of my positive Know moods that had come suddenly upon me, when there was no doubt about our future when, although there was nothing to show for it in our immediate surroundings, I had the greatest confidence that we were on the road to warmth, food and happiness. In no small part I knew this was due to the infectious enthusiasm and confidence of Jem; but at the same time I thought that the salty sea breeze had more than a little to do with it.

Mr. Bowler had suddenly stopped. He was balancing himself precariously on the path.

" What's up? " said Jem impatiently. He was a few yards

66

farther on but had stopped when he heard Mr. Bowler give a grunt. We were so far down the cliff path now that the swirling water seemed to be about our feet. Mr. Bowler had turned round and was looking out to sea. He made no answer but stretched out his arm and pointed. I had to stand up to see and for the briefest flash I saw a light some distance out to sea. Then it was gone and the night seemed all the darker for our having seen it.

The news excited Jem tremendously. " Where? Which direction? " he insisted.

" Look, there it is again."

A small orange eye appeared and pricked out again. Jem gave a sort of half cheer and slithered wildly down what remained of the cliff path. " Come on," he cried and began to run along the beach, running across the ribbed sand, keeping well under the shadow of the cliff so that we soon lost sight of him.

Mr. Bowler, it seemed, was quite determined to remain unexcited. While he waited for Jack White to slither down the few remaining feet of the cliff path, he was occupied in brushing his clothes with his hand, slowly raising and stretching first his right leg and then his left leg, complaining that so much exercise gave him aches and pains and then saying he could not imagine why we had not gone to the cabin. I noticed that Jack White was shivering with cold. Although I looked I could no longer see the light out at sea. We made our way along the beach in the direction that Jem had taken and soon became aware of a great deal of activity going on. Figures seemed to be scurrying between the face of the cliff and the water's edge but as the cliff here cast the beach into a great shadow, it was not possible to profit by the moonlight and make out what was going on.

Jem was immediately back by our side, changed into a

different being by excitement it seemed, for he was almost incoherent. "Friends, friends, friends, but first you must be looked after. Ah! My—Marlow, where are you? Marlow, I say." And then turning to us once more. "You see, things turn out well in the long run. We've got friends I tell you. O-ho, now we shall——" and he drove his fist into the palm of his right hand.

In answer to his cry, a short, thick-set man, almost a hunchback, came lumbering over and stood regarding us with what I thought was a great deal of suspicion.

"Take them into the cave," snapped Jem. "Food, something hot and clothes. Above all, clothes for the negro." Then Jem was away, racing down to the surf where, my eyes now having got more accustomed to the gloom, I could see that a boat was half dragged out of the water and a group of men were unloading a number of boxes and packages. Jem was throwing his arms about and occasionally giving a little skip in the air. If it were not for the great need for silence (the work was being carried out so as to avoid arousing the curiosity of any strangers who might be passing), I felt that he would be shouting for pure joy at the top of his voice; something had clearly happened for which he had been waiting a long time. He was triumphant.

Marlow, the deformed little man, hurried us over to the mouth of the cave which could be clearly seen because there were lights inside. Men were coming and going, carrying sacks and boxes, but we were not given very much time to have a look at them. In front of the cave the sand was as clean and smooth as in the bar-parlour of an inn but the air was chill and cold as though there were quantities of ice stored in the rocks. The cave was about twelve feet across at the opening but very low indeed, so that we had to stoop to go in. Mr. Bowler grunted and complained bitterly. It seemed that a cool breeze came out of the cave itself, blowing from the innermost recesses. It howled mournfully like an autumn gale in the chimney of an old house and even then I remembered thinking that this meant there must be another way out of the cave apart from the shore entrance. To begin with, we found ourselves in a small cave which served rather as the entrance hall to a house, for there were a number of chambers and passages leading off. A hurricane lamp was flickering and swinging from the ceiling. I was now so tired that I was ready to lie down on the floor of the cave and go to sleep there. The negro boxer stood looking round in amazement, shivering with cold, gathering his dressing-gown closer to him, and looking very much out of place in our strange surroundings. Marlow impatiently ushered us along one of the side passages, not one of the passages along which the men were bearing whatever it was the boat had brought, illuminated by an occasional hurricane lamp. We soon found ourselves climbing, for the floor rose quite steeply. Now and again a patch of stone would flash like a jeweller's shop. Afterwards, I found that this was caused by mica and rock crystals catching and reflecting the light like so much glass. I looked back the way we had come and even then, in the obscurity where the light from the hurricane lamps did not penetrate, there were stones shining phosphorescently in the dark. Marlow took a sudden turn to the right along a side-passage which seemed to bring up sheer against a wall of rock but instead there was another sharp left turn.

" Like going into a Chinaman's house," said Mr. Bowler. " It may be of interest to you to know that they build their houses like this because bad spirits can't turn corners."

We were in a room in the bowels of the cliff. It was a furnished room with a real table and chairs, lit by an oil lamp that was suspended by three fine chains from a huge spike that was wedged in the ceiling. We looked about us.

"Make yourselves at home," said the sinister Marlow, grinning at us in a conspiratorial way, and Mr. Bowler immediately subsided into a large basket chair that screeched like a cat whenever he moved.

The room was perhaps fifteen feet long by as many broad, very crudely cut out of the stone, for this was no natural cave. I imagined that this was some old smuggler's depot and the very thought reminded me of the oddness of Jem's behaviour. I was too tired really to follow up any line of thought but it did occur to me with considerable force that Jem might not be as honest as he appeared, that all his talk about having lost his memory might be lies, and that his real activity was this of smuggling.

In one corner of the room was a camp-bed with a pillow, two blankets and some sheets. Around the small but heavy-looking table were three ordinary kitchen chairs. Behind Mr. Bowler's basket chair were three stone jars containing, as we discovered afterwards, a supply of drinking water. A half a dozen biscuit tins and something that looked like a fisherman's net made up the rest of the furnishings of this surprising apartment. Jack White seemed quite overcome. He sat on the table, hunched in his dressing-gown, swinging his legs backwards and forwards, whistling softly to himself.

As soon as Marlow had gone, the negro looked round him and said, "Speaking for myself, sirs, I don't like this at all. It's my opinion that something strictly illegal is going on."

But when Marlow and another man returned bearing a shining bucket of hot soup, a basket of small loaves, dishes

and spoons, we forgot our apprehensions and ate heartily. Marlow stood watching us, looking keenly into our faces as though he was trying to fix them in his memory. His assistant, a thin youth of about twenty or so, wearing navy-blue trousers and a grey jersey, reappeared carrying similar clothes in his hands. They were for Jack White who put them on in great delight. They were a little small for him but he was so pleased he became almost jovial in contrast with his previous moods, when he could think of nothing to say but, " I'm the most miserable man since Job."

Mr. Bowler, too, seemed very pleased with himself. " If I may be allowed to express myself, I should say this. Life is a battle. But not a battle in the ordinary sense of the word and you can do yourself a considerable amount of harm by being combative. That is the mistake of our impetuous young friend, Jem. Life must be—well, it must be understood! It must be weighed up. You must assess its advantages and disadvantages. Then, when you have found the weak spot—go for it with all your strength. At the moment, we are at a special disadvantage. We, with the exception of our pugilist friend, do not know who we are."

I saw Jack White start at this but Mr. Bowler went on. "Therefore we have to be extra specially careful in our watching and waiting. The man who may appear to be our friend may be our enemy. And the man who may appear to be our enemy may be our friend. Step carefully, eat what is given us, sleep where we can, keep our eyes open, that's our programme." I could see that he was casting eyes on the camp bed.

"Who's lost his memory?" Jack White asked.

"Myself, this young gentleman and the young rogue who stepped into the boxing ring with you—or he says he has." Mr. Bowler took his whistle out of his pocket. "I can't really understand how I came into possession of this, for example, and I play it shockingly badly."

I think we all felt better as a result of the soup. We had barely finished when Jem himself came in rubbing his hands and asking us whether we had everything we wanted. Mr. Bowler immediately said yes, except an insufficiency of beds, so Jem had blankets brought in, said that as Mr. Bowler was the oldest, he could sleep on the camp bed but that the rest of us would have to curl up on the floor in the blankets. This Jack White and I immediately prepared to do, for although I was dying to ask Jem what everything meant, my eyes persisted in closing themselves and they remained open long enough only to see that Jem had no intentions of going to sleep yet. He saw that we were settled and immediately went out again. Although I was so tired, I did not sleep soundly and all through the night I was aware of the tramp of feet, the coming and going of Jem, the flashing of lights and a cold that seemed to gnaw at my bones. Then silence and deep sleep.

The first thing I was aware of when waking was Jack White standing in the middle of the floor swaying backwards and forwards and holding his head.

Mr. Bowler was still asleep.

"What's the matter?" I asked.

He looked at me as though I was a complete stranger.

"Who are you?" he asked. "Where am I? Who am I?"

I rolled back my blankets and rose to my feet with a feeling of terror, of having come in touch with the unknown, the mysterious, the completely inexplicable.

I looked at Mr. Bowler and noticed that he was still wearing his hat.

PART TWO

CHAPTER V

AN ENEMY AMONG US

QUITE absurdly I lost my temper. "You're Jack White, you're Jack White!" I shouted at the top of my voice. "Look at yourself. You're Jack White the boxer. Don't you remember? How can you say that you don't remember? It's rubbish. You're only trying to scare us, that's what you're doing. Look at me, don't you remember?"

"Who are you?" he repeated, I thought, woodenly and stupidly. We had awakened Mr. Bowler but he made no move. His eyes were open. He lay there regarding us, his face wedged between the top of the blanket and his bowler hat. I went over and shook him by the shoulder, saying that something devilish was happening, that the negro had lost his memory, that I felt we were all in a kind of prison. Mr. Bowler threw back the blanket and climbed with some difficulty out of the creaking bed. He did not seem at all surprised and this fact endeared him to me. He was still wearing his clothes, apparently having thought it too cold to go to bed without them.

75

"Good morning, gentlemen," he said a little mournfully and his eye roamed around the rock-hewn room. "I can't say as I'm really surprised. There's a nasty sort of atmosphere about this place. Where's that young criminal?" I knew that he meant Jem.

I felt Jack White's presence in the room as a strange abnormality. To my imagination, he was not so much a man who had lost his memory, as an animal, a piece of machinery almost, that had suddenly spoken and shown itself to be gifted with a sub-human intelligence.

"Shut up," said Mr. Bowler suddenly and I realised that I had been gabbling away in a wild attempt to prove that the negro was deceiving us. It even occurred to me that the fact of our having told him, the night before, that we ourselves had lost our memories, had been playing on his mind. During sleep, or in that terrible time between sleep and waking when ideas and events spin, mouth like monsters, gabble like demons, the idea of forgetfulness might have seized upon the negro like some foul parasite and turned his mind. Or perhaps he had taken a chill through walking in the cold night air and was really ill.

Jack White was looking from Mr. Bowler to me with an air of the greatest distrust. Then his eyes wandered round the room, looking at the table, the chairs, the vats of water, the fishing net, as though these objects might give him some clue to his identity.

Then I realised that it was not the negro of whom I was frightened. I was frightened of myself. It would be a wild exaggeration to say that the fact of my loss of memory had ever been absent from my mind. But it was an idea to which I had grown more or less accustomed. I had been fortunate in meeting Mr. Bowler and Jem so soon after realising the strangeness of my situation; the calmness of the one and the cheerfulness of the other had given me courage. Then, things had been happening. We had been to a fair, we had had excitement. But now that the black boxer had been afflicted in the same way, it seemed that the true horror of the situation struck me for the first time. I felt as though my eyes were bandaged and I was in a forest of wild beasts. I did not know from which direction the attack would come. I did not know when I should feel the teeth, the claws, the savage attack of my enemy. For this reason, Jack White himself was a monster in my eyes. He was like some strange animal seen in a nightmare, some beast that presses closer and closer until his breath is burning upon your face.

Mr. Bowler was talking quietly and earnestly to the negro. He was telling him that there was absolutely nothing to be afraid of. "You are with friends, Mr. White," he said, "and you can trust us. We understand what has happened to you perfectly. If you trust us you will soon find that everything is quite all right. The important thing at the moment is to wash and then find something to eat. I'm hungry. Can't hear anybody about, can you, Roger? All that hullabaloo in the night. I don't know how they expect honest people to sleep."

By some means, Mr. Bowler's bravely spoken words had a calming effect upon me and for the first time I could begin to reason about our situation. Jack White, I saw, was not to be feared. All his physical strength, his fine body, remained to him, but the true strength of a man, his knowledge of the world and his position in it, had been filched away. He was weak and helpless and I realised that it was our duty to do all in our power to help him. My imagination now transformed him into an ineffective, innocent, kitten-like creature and myself correspondingly large and masterful. With all my heart I was sorry for him.

"I feel like as though I was walking through a thick mist," he said solemnly. "What is this strange place?"

"Don't think," said Mr. Bowler, "unless you consider what you would like for breakfast. I wonder what the service in this hotel is like."

"I feel as though I was dead and yet not dead," said the negro. "There is wickedness in the world."

There was the sound of boots rattling over the loose pebbles of the passage outside and a moment later Jem entered. Seen in the light of the hurricane lamp, he gave the air of being physically tired but, at the same time, as alert and cheerful as ever. His eyes were red but they switched from the one to the other of us rapidly. It was quite clear that he had had little, if any, sleep that night.

"Things are going well, very well," he said. "We've got in enough supplies to last us for a couple of months."

"Young man," said Mr. Bowler firmly, "we feel that the time for a complete explanation has come. We have allowed you to lead us by the nose quite enough and I think, me being the oldest and consequently knowing more than you do, that it is now my turn to do a bit of planning."

Jem looked a little taken aback by this but he said nothing. He stood with his legs wide apart, his hands thrust into his trousers pocket.

"To go back a long way," continued Mr. Bowler, giving each word due emphasis, as though he were a lawyer framing a criminal charge, "I should like to know how you came to be in possession of my trousers. I didn't lose my memory wearing football shorts. But that's a long way back and there are other and perhaps more important questions to discuss. The point is that I consider it is time that I began to use my authority."

"What authority?" said Jem with a grin.

" The natural authority of age and experience."

" You forget that I am older than you. My memory goes back farther than yours. I was attacked by the enemy before you. That is the only thing that counts. My rights as leader are unquestionable. I have power because I know more about the really important things. The really important things," he repeated with great emphasis but still not moving from his original position. " I understand the enemy. I know the way he thinks and the way he moves. I understand his mind. I can tell you what he is going to do before he does it. The right of leadership is mine because I am the strongest." He looked at Jack White. " Not physically, Jackie. You're the toughest looking bird I've seen for a long time. I am strong because I know. Knowledge is strength. You can ask any one of the gang you will see working in these caves. They serve me blindly because they have confidence in me. They are all men, like you and me, and like Roger there, whom the enemy has attacked; and they know the only chance they have of defeating the enemy is to do as I tell them, when I tell them, where I tell them. You will find our organisation here quite a military affair. Like being in a kind of army. Anything less than that would be useless. We are an army fighting the most unscrupulous and dangerous enemy that man has ever come up against. And it is because I realise this fact more clearly than anybody else that the leadership is mine. I am the leader."

His voice had been rising. What had begun as a simple sort of explanation, a defence almost, became at the end a speech.

Jack White looked at him in bewilderment. I felt stirred. I was convinced of the truth of everything that Jem had said. Only Mr. Bowler seemed unimpressed.

"Young man, you have a rare power over us for the time being. But if it is true what you say about knowing what the enemy is going to do before he does it, then there is no need for us to tell you what has happened now." He looked at Jem closely.

"What do you mean?" Jem looked about him quickly, as though he feared seeing one of the policemen, one of the enemy that is, lurking in the room.

"You see," said Mr. Bowler in triumph. "What did I tell you? You don't know. Jack White here has lost his memory."

In the silence that followed I could hear, somewhere, the drip of water; the cavern was damp and some moist rock was oozing water.

"Is this true?" demanded Jem.

"I feel as though the brain has been taken out of me," said Jack White.

"But this is impossible, impossible!" shouted Jem in a fury. "You haven't been out of our sight. A policeman has come nowhere near you. You are trying to fool me."

"It is true," I said. Only then did Jem believe.

"I once thought," he said bitterly, "that they worked with poison. I thought we could defend ourselves against them by ordinary means. I thought that a locked door could keep them out, keep them out, that is, until we were ready to launch our offensive. Now I see that they have more fiendish means than I had thought. They can attack us from a distance. That means that none of us is safe. Even me. They can rob me of this little, precious drop of knowledge and then all will be lost."

"We mustn't lose our heads," I said.

"The thought that they can attack us here in our own fortress!" he exclaimed.

"You young rascal," said Mr. Bowler in a truly thunder-ous voice. "You may be able to take in a mere boy but you can't deceive me. It is my belief that there is no enemy. You are the monster at the bottom of all this—this bestiality. Who else could it be? I refuse to believe that anyone could rob a man of his memory at a distance. To make a man forget, you've got to use drugs and drugs have to be put in drinks or thrust into a man's arm with a needle. There is no magic about it. I don't believe in magic. You know a sight more about what's going on than you'd like to admit. What is this boat lying off the shore? Yes, and all these stores? Where do they come from? Who pays for them? Is it likely that a poor half-wit like you—you say that you lost your memory a short while ago—how is it that you can get this great organisation going, this cave fitted out, chairs, tables. I don't believe you. I don't believe that the enemy exists. At least, it would be more accurate to say that you are the enemy. Now, am I right?" And refusing to listen to what Jem had to say, he went stumping round the room, muttering about his having been humiliated in the first place by the fact that his trousers were stolen; and it struck him as mighty queer that Jem should suddenly turn up with them.

So Jem ignored him and turned to Jack White. "Jack, old chap, you've got to listen to me. I'm terribly sorry for what has happened. There is no doubt about it, I should have been more on my guard. We must never relax. Watch all the time and never give way an instant. Well, if it was due to my carelessness, then I owe it to you to put you on your feet again. You understand?"

"No," said the negro.

"There are a group of men in this country," explained Jem, "who are trying to gain control of it by trickery.

They have some poison that robs a man of his memory. When they have reduced the whole population in this way, they'll triumph. They'll be able to do just what they want. See? They got at you, though I don't know how." He went on to explain the idea of the ruthless police force who would stop at nothing to carry out this plan; at the same time they were on thin ice because there was a move to do away with them. He explained that the ordinary people resented the existence of the police force because there was no crime in the country and therefore the police were thought of as simply a waste of good money. "It is the common people we must help," explained Jem. "But the first important thing is this." Here he gave Mr. Bowler a very stern look. "You must have confidence in me. That is the only thing that keeps our ship together. United we stand, divided we fall. If we destroy ourselves by suspicions, accusations, doubts, then we are the stupidest lunatics ever created. When I tell you to do something you must forget that it is I, an individual giving an order. We are all equals here. The order really comes from you yourselves. You are obeying yourself. But without this discipline we shall certainly fail. Do you understand? "

"I protest," said Mr. Bowler.

"I am very sorry. I am disappointed in you. It's only your silly pride that is preventing you from seeing things as they really are. You don't like it because, as you say, I'm much younger than you are. You don't like taking orders from me. Well, you will have to be looked after until you do." He went to the doorway and shouted for Marlow.

"It is no such thing," said Mr. Bowler indignantly. "I accuse you of being a rogue and a liar. I accuse you of creating bogey-men which do not exist. What you want is a good spanking."

"All right," said Jem as the sinister Marlow, the youth whom we had seen the night before, and another taller man with a thin red beard appeared. At once they seized the astonished Mr. Bowler and, in spite of his energetic resistance, hustled him out of the cave.

"What are they going to do with him?" I cried in indignation.

"Don't worry," said Jem. "He will be well treated."

"But you have no right to treat him like that."

"Do you really think so?" There was a gentle note in his voice. I knew that Jem liked me. "Don't you see that he could ruin all our plans? Before very long, we shall be taking action against the police. When the campaign really begins, a man like Mr. Bowler could ruin us. Don't you see? Don't you trust me?"

I thought for a moment. I had been shocked by the way Mr. Bowler had been rushed away but once I began to consider it as a necessity I realised that personal considerations, even the fondness that one man might have for another, were not so very important.

"Yes," I said. "I trust you."

"That's fine," said Jem slapping me on the back. "And you, Jackie—for you are Jackie, you know. Are you going to let me try and sort things out? I understand, you see."

There was no expression on the negro's face. "I feel alone and helpless," he said.

"No, not alone. It's a fine morning outside, though you wouldn't think so in here. The sea is—well, I'm going for a swim before breakfast. What do you say?"

"Oh, it'll be cold," I said.

Jem's enthusiasm, as always, was infectious. We found that Jack White could not be stirred out of the melancholy that had overwhelmed him; so Jem gave orders for his

83

breakfast to be brought in. Then he and I stripped and walked down the corridor to the sea, walking tenderly for the pebbles cut the soles of my feet. I was shivering with cold, but Jem seemed to radiate heat. We arrived at the smooth sand of the entrance cave and although I looked about me, I could see no sign of the cargo that had been unloaded the night before. Then out into the brilliant sun, so brilliant that I was dazzled after the obscurity of the cave. An enormous green sea was folding itself neatly up in creamy rollers on the yellow beach. Seagulls whirled and cried, settling on the waves, rising and falling with the swell. There was no sign of a boat lying off-shore, nothing to show for the orange light that we had seen the night before.

"Ee-eh!" screeched Jem and set off running for the sea. Without any hesitation he plunged into the surf, waded as far out as he could and then, over went his arm and he was swimming.

The sea was icy and snatched all the breath out of my

body. The surf roared about my ears and, seeing an enormous wave coming towards me, I ducked my head, and the whole green world of water was about me. Then I was through, snatching mouthfuls of air, buoyed up marvellously on the swell of foaming water, drawn forward and lifted up the receding wave and then smothered by an advancing wave. But I was through the surf, out in deeper water, striking out after Jem's head, finding a warm undercurrent that tickled my legs deliciously. Not knowing whether there were any treacherous currents, I did not attempt to go out too far. I turned over on my back and looked up at the sun, the blue sky, small clouds like pigeons; then back, between my feet, at the red cliff rising and falling like some great ship.

Jem was at my side. " Back," he said. He flipped his hand in the direction of the shore and, quietly, we swam back until we began to feel the backwash and put our feet down to fight against the force of the water.

In contrast, the sun felt warm and we sat on the beach for a while, saying nothing. Looking at Jem, I could not believe that he planned any harm for Mr. Bowler and, going back to breakfast, I began to feel that things were going very well indeed.

Now events are going to start moving, I thought. Jem gathered together his band of workers and introduced Jack White and myself to them. Although there were only three of them, Jem insisted on their standing in a row at attention like soldiers while he spoke to them. The only one of the three whose name I knew was the stunted man called Marlow; the youth who had brought in clothes for Jack White was, it appeared, called Henry; and the man with the thin beard was called, quite simply, Red, because of its colour. Henry was roughly the same age as Jem but the other two must have been considerably older. I was very much impressed by the great respect with which they listened to Jem's words of introduction.

After telling them our names, or the name which I had been given and the black boxer's true name, Jem went on to talk brightly and cheerfully of the difficulties that lay in our way. He suddenly broke off, gave me a look and then said I had better fall into line with the others, me and Jack White. I did so eagerly because I had learned the necessity for discipline; Jack White followed more slowly like a great puzzled dog.

" Perhaps you will think," said Jem, " that a boy will not be much help to us, but you can take it from me that a boy can do things and go into places without suspicion, which perhaps you and me could not. Roger's a good lad, you can take it from me and you've only got to take a look at Jackie to know that we've had a rare stroke of luck."

We were standing in the mouth of the cave. The sunlight fell obliquely across the opening, warming our backs. Jem stood in the shadow. To me he seemed magnificent, youthful, gay, confident. " Thanks to your excellent work last night, we have got in enough stores to last us a good while. When the others arrive they will be grateful."

I suppose I must have looked surprised at this reference to the others for he said immediately, " You don't imagine that we few are the only ones the enemy has attacked? " I remembered that he had spoken of about twenty. " The number is actually very great but the number I have been able to gather together is eighteen. It is safer for all of us not to be in the same place. There are other hiding places known to me alone." I soon learned that Jem was the only person who thoroughly understood his own organisation. It appeared that there were two other groups who came to this cavern periodically to take supplies, which consisted entirely of food, and to receive orders. He took complete responsibility upon his shoulders and had confidence in nobody.

Then he dismissed the parade in military style and told Henry, Red and Marlow to go and get some sleep. In the afternoon he would have more news for us. In the meantime, Jack White and I were not to leave the cave area.

I was glad of the opportunity to talk to the negro for I knew that I could be of the greatest service to Jem by making sure that he completely understood the situation. As soon as we were left alone, I went over to where he had stretched himself on the sand in the sun and began asking him how he felt. He showed me his large white teeth in a smile but it was the smile a man will give to conceal pain.

" At least the food is good," he remarked.

" But you understand what has happened? We are all in the same boat here? " But my own anger with the policemen was nothing to Jack's. All this time it seemed that he had been turning the treachery over and over in his mind.

" I shall kill them with my naked hands," he said quietly.

It seemed that the loss of his memory had frozen the black boxer; now he was just beginning to thaw out and he was a different man from the peace-loving pugilist who had been shocked by the barbarity of his profession; certainly a different man from the silent, bewildered creature who had refused to come swimming. He sprang to his feet.

" Where are they, that's what I want to know. What are we waiting here for? Why don't we make a beginning? Where is this—this——"

" Jem," I suggested.

" Where is he? "

Jem had gone into the cave with the others, presumably

to rest after the night's work. I said as much and, to my astonishment, Jack White immediately dashed into the cave. I suppose he had the idea of looking for Jem. I hurried after, crying after him to stop. It occurred to me that the system of caves might be more complicated than I had thought; there might be treacherous holes in the ground, rifts, pools of water. But the negro went on. His fury drove him. I wanted to explain that we must have sufficient confidence in Jem to wait for his orders but I knew that the negro would not, at this moment, listen to reasoning like this.

He hurried up the rising corridor to the room where we had spent the night. I came to the entrance just as he was coming out and was hurled back against the rocky wall by his arm. I was severely winded but made some attempt to catch at the back of his jersey. His fist came round and he was off back down the corridor to explore the other side passages. He began shouting as he went. He cried out wanting to know where Jem was and the whole honeycomb of caves and linking corridors caught up his voice, hollowed it, echoed it and finally choked it away in a lingering sigh.

By the time I had reached the entrance cave, he had once more disappeared up one of the other two branching corridors. The echoes were so confused that I could not decide which of the two corridors he had taken. The sound of the pad-pad of his feet (he was still wearing his boxing pumps) was multiplied a dozen times as though a pride of lions were exploring this underground lair. The cries began once more. They seemed to bubble through depths of water and then waver crazily as though the negro's body were being shaken by a violent fever; but it was as though fifteen men were crying. Even as I stood there, undecided which passage to take, the cries came to a sudden stop. For a moment there was a silence in which the solid red rock of the cliff appeared to be vibrating like a bell. Then the rock was speaking (for this is how it seemed to me) with a frailer, thinner voice, but as angry as the whining of a mosquito. I realised that this was Jem. The rock vibrated with his vehemence. From Jack White there came not a word. Then, once more the tingling silence. Finally, the lion-like pad-pad and Jack White came rushing down the left-hand corridor, past me without a glance, his face rigid as though carved out of wood, and out into the sunlight where he threw himself face down on the sand. By now the tide had come in considerably. The negro had thrown himself almost at the edge of the water and even as I watched, a wave broke and sent a cascade of water boiling around his head. He dragged himself wearily back from the water and lay on his back gazing up at the sky.

"Jack," I said. "We must keep calm. I'm sure that everything will turn out all right."

He spat at me like a big cat. "Get to hell," he cried. "Get to hell out of my sight."

CHAPTER VI

WE PREPARE FOR THE STRUGGLE

THIS WAS the routine. Breakfast soon after the sun was up and usually, although not every morning, a swim. My body had hardened to the coldness of the water and I even took pleasure in the fish-like numbness that attacked me when I bore through the surf to the oily rise and fall of waves farther out. Sometimes we bathed, Henry, Red, Jack White, Jem and myself, when the red sun was balancing on the watery horizon, when the day was raw. Blood-coloured waves licked at my flanks as I turned over to float; the red cliffs seemed to be fired from within and the sands, pale yellow in ordinary light, were the colour of honey because of the warm blush suffused over them. Marlow seemed permanently excused from this morning bathe. He occupied himself with the preparation of breakfast in any case. After about five minutes, Jem would raise his arm, flip it back towards the beach and say, " Back." All of us, Jack White included who obeyed orders with an astonishing meekness, turned and made for the beach. We passed round a great hairy towel to dry ourselves. Then hot milkless tea and bread.

We looked for stones. Although the sand was flat and pure, under the cliff itself were pebbles in profusion. Jem would pick up a curiously shaped pebble, a kidney-shaped pebble, or one shaped like a pear, and tell us that

we had to gather a hundred that were exactly the same. On occasion, he would say that the exact shape did not matter. We had to find white pebbles ribbed with brown; or amber-coloured fragments that glowed when you held them between your eye and the sun. And we would, after a morning's search, place our pebbles in a heap outside the mouth of the cave. The procedure was always exactly the same. When the sun was at its highest in the sky, Jem would emerge from the cave where he had been busy on some job of his own that he would never talk about and on which, in any case, we would never dare to question him. He would inspect our pebbles while we stood at attention behind them, our fingers pressed to the side of our calves, as far down as we could reach. Before we had our mid-day meal, Jem would carefully examine these stones, giving the impression that he was looking for a particular stone. This did not prevent him from being sarcastic when he came across a pebble that was obviously different from the others. He insisted on the pebbles looking exactly the same. " It isn't so much the number. The size of the pile is not very important. What is important, is that they should be as like as peas in a pod. Look at this thing. Stand forward the man who brought this in? "

Usually it was Red. He said his eyes were weak and he could not tell the difference between the pebbles very well. He pleaded to be given other work. In vain. Jem whipped him with his tongue and said that a man was only a man if he overcame his defects. Everything comes to the man who is patient and courageous he said.

" Perhaps there are times when you feel sorry for yourselves. Not a bit of it. Look at me. Do I look sorry for myself? I am in the same corner as you. But a man with a wooden leg walks faster than an ordinary man. A man who stutters says more than you and me. And because we are lame in our minds "—he looked into our faces one by one—" because we have forgotten and no longer regret our memories, we are going to whip ourselves on to great things. Your eyes are weak." To Red. " Good. Use your fingers to feel. Develop your sense of touch so that it replaces your sight. Never, never, never admit defeat."

He picked up the pebble that didn't match and threw it over our heads out to sea. We heard it plump in. A pause. We stood waiting to be dismissed.

" It's true, isn't it? " asked Jem. " We no longer regret that we do not remember. Do you regret, Red? "

" No," said Red.

" And you? " Henry said no.

I was standing next to Jack White and felt the struggle going on inside him as distinctly as I could feel the beach beneath my feet vibrating under the thunder of the surf.

" No," he said.

It was hard to answer in any other way. But I was quite sincere when I uttered my ' No ', too. Mr. Bowler had been shut away and although I was sorry about it, there was no denying that it had been necessary; and apart from that one regret, there was nothing in our way of life that did not bring me the keenest pleasure. When the battle against the enemy was won and, presumably, our memories were restored, there was always the chance of a great disappointment. I was sure of the happiness that I was now enjoying. I was coming to fear recovering my memory as we will always fear the unknown.

Jem had asked me last. I don't know whether it was my imagination but he seemed to be more pleased with my ' No ' than with any of the others. Perhaps, as I was the youngest, he felt more responsibility for me. There was always a note of greater friendliness in the way he spoke to me, he was always a little more gentle than with any of the others.

After the midday meal of tinned meat, boiled potatoes and oranges, we were given the job of throwing all the pebbles we had gathered, back into the sea.

In the afternoon we climbed the cliffs. We were always trying to find new and more dangerous routes for getting to the top. In my own case, Jem insisted on a gentle breaking in. I had to climb, descend and climb the ordinary path time after time before he would let me attempt even the simplest of the other ascents. And then he went on in front of me, showing me the footholds, the convenient tough roots growing in the seams of the rock, and the tiny ledges where there was just room to walk and balance, always provided that you had a handhold as well. We prided ourselves on making the climb without the use of ropes and Jem would have been furious with any of the others if he had seen them so much as giving each other a helping hand. But for me he would sometimes stretch down his hand and tell me to catch hold. I did not have a good head for heights and the occasional glimpses of the tiny waves crawling up a minute beach, perhaps a hundred feet below, would make my head spin; because of this, I was always glad of any help that he was prepared to give me although, when we had safely made the top and were lying on our stomachs to watch the progress of the others, I used to regret that I had accepted his help. It used to humiliate me. I swore that the next time I would do the climb absolutely without any help from him. But it was terribly difficult.

I could only imagine that in all this Jem was training us in toughness for the struggle which was to come. What struggle? Somehow I did not imagine it as a struggle in which guns or other weapons would be used. I did not think it would be so simple as that. We were, in some way I as yet did not understand, going to fight with our minds. I had seen no sign of any weapons in the cave. If we were to use them, surely Jem would have arranged for us to practise with them. It occurred to me that the complexities of the struggle were too much for me to understand. This gave me all the more confidence in our leader.

But I had made an enemy and a very dangerous one at that, too. It was Marlow. I had never liked the distorted little man who rarely spoke to me except when he was forced to utter a yes or no. With Red and Henry I could talk about unimportant things, subjects which had nothing to do with the struggle or the enemy; food, the weather, the appearance of the sea. But Marlow either could never bring himself to think of me as having sufficient importance to talk to; or he was continually taken up with his dark thoughts about the police. But he avoided me. I did not know at the time but I later understood that he was violently jealous of the way Jem treated me.

Jem suddenly gave up the afternoon climbing, saying that he had to busy himself on more important matters. But we others had to continue. And I found myself climbing near Marlow up a sort of chimney in the rock with one side open to the sea. The others, Jack White, Henry and Red, were making the ascent farther along the cliff. Marlow and I were alone. He could climb like a monkey and had been working his way up the chimney by setting his back against one side, his feet against the other and levering himself up as easily as though he was going up stairs. The chimney was no more than twelve feet high but it was the only way of getting past a swelling out of the cliff. It was sixty feet above the beach. It needed a cool head, perhaps a little more strength than I had and the sort of awful patience that makes you content with progress of fractions of an inch.

I waited for Marlow to get to the top of the chimney and settle himself on a ledge before attempting the climb myself. The width of the chimney was just a little too much for me to get a great deal of leverage with my legs and this placed such a strain upon me that by the time I had climbed halfway, I found myself slipping. I dared not look down. If I slipped, the ledge from which I had started, was so narrow that I should not be able to get sufficient foothold before pitching over and out. I should crash on to the beach. It was just at the moment when I was feeling that I could go neither forward nor back, when I felt a small pebble strike me on the back of the neck. To begin with, I thought that it might have been accidentally dislodged by Marlow but when another and another followed, I realised that he was deliberately dropping them.

" Stop it! For God's sake, stop it! " I said between my teeth. " I'm slipping."

The only answer was another stone which struck me painfully on the knee. I heard Marlow laughing.

" Do you want to murder me? " I said. The effort of talking was exhausting. Marlow was laughing continually. The sound seemed to meet with some obstruction in his throat and come in choked gasps. Then he spoke, making the longest speech on record so far.

"A little, tiny, insignificant boy. A child." And another choking laugh. If anything, I was taller than Marlow and it occurred to me that he resented the fact. But there was a bitter taste in my mouth and I felt tears running down the back of my throat. Another stone caught me on the crown of the head. I was slipping and there was nothing that could save me. My limbs were taut. It seemed that I had no more control over them than if I had been taken by a cramp in swimming; and, indeed, that is just what this was, a sort of cramp.

The wind that had been gently breathing around us all the way up in our climb, now became stronger. I felt it pressing round me with such strength that it even relieved me a little of the weight of my own body, lifting me a little. Of course, this effect was very slight but such was the strain on my legs that I was glad of even this relief.

Another pebble struck me on the crown of the head. I had quite made up my mind that Marlow meant to destroy me and just at the moment when I could see no hope for myself, just when I felt my strength was going, a wave of anger flowed through my body, I took hold of myself once more and said that where I had come up I could go down. The main reason for my helplessness I decided was an unwillingness to allow my head and shoulders to sink lower than the level of my feet. The burst of anger had cleared my head. I realised that I was not going to get out of the chimney unless I could find some firmer grip for my hands, thus preventing my body from slipping farther. Keeping my legs fixed, my feet planted against the wall opposite, I began to wriggle my body lower and lower, straightening out my legs gradually as I did so. I felt the wind pressing around me like a friend. Marlow was now crumbling soft sandstone between his fingers and allowing the dust to drain down on my head; this meant I had to keep my eyes closed. If I did not find a break in the rock with my fingers, some root, a hold of some sort, then I felt that I should slip and go head-first over the edge. Strangely enough, I felt no fear now. I was quite calm. I had come to the limit. My legs were stretched out straight and no longer gave me any purchase on the rock. I stretched down with my fingers. Cold flat rock. Nothing. Then I knew that I could not hold on.

I heard a voice calling up from the beach below. I dared not open my mouth to reply or turn my head down to see.

"Ahoy there! What are you waiting for? Get a move on." The wind bore the words up. It was Jem and the relief that this piece of knowledge gave me, brought about such a relaxation of my body that I almost slipped. Jem was watching us. At least it would be impossible for Marlow to continue with the dropping of his stones and dust now. He had indeed stopped laughing, but faithful to the rules of the game, he was making no effort to give me a helping hand. I could hear his boots grating on the rock above. He was taking Jem at his word and continuing his climb. I began to feel sick with fatigue. Even as the wind billowed up and supported me, there were moments when it drew back like an outgoing wave, drawing me away from the face of the cliff. I could not, could not hold on. My body had become as hard and rigid as stone, had become stone itself; I had grown incorporate with the cliff and I had no more power to move it than I had power to move the solid mass of the cliff itself. There was an increasing bitterness in my mouth. Although my eyes were firmly closed, I felt light and shade passing over them, as though sea birds were wheeling in front of my face. I was slipping. Quite for no reason at all, I began to think of Mr. Bowler. My mind was in the sort of daze that takes it in fever. I was hardly aware of what was real and what was unreal. Mr. Bowler in his rock prison, I thought. Then it was as though the sound of his whistle was coming from very close at hand, as though I had my ear clamped to the wall of his prison and he were vainly trying to attract the attention of the world by his music. The whistling died away and I heard the roaring in my ears of the blood stream that coursed around my body.

At that moment, I heard boots on the rock face and arms took me from beneath. "All right, son. You're all right now." It was Jem, by some miracle borne up from the beach sixty feet below to my help. Of course, he must have begun the climb as soon as he saw I was in real difficulties. He supported me to the bottom of the chimney, where he tied a rope around my waist. He did not say a word and I felt that he was angry with me. He insisted on my making the descent first, he followed after, the rope taut between us to prevent me from slipping. We went down very slowly. At every moment I was getting back breath and blood. I was beginning to use my limbs as though they really belonged to me. I was losing the sense that they had turned to stone; once more they were flesh and blood. At the bottom of the cliff I stood unsteadily on my feet, feeling that the weight of my body was too great to be supported.

Jem sprang down the last few feet, bringing a small avalanche of rubble with him.

" Marlow tried to kill me," I said. " He threw stones at me. I should have climbed the chimney but for that. He tried to kill me I say." I knew that the important thing now was to explain my failure. This was a test that I had not passed.

Jem sat on a boulder and looked at me seriously.

" It does not matter to me whether what you say is true or not. If Marlow tried to kill you, that is your affair. It is not mine. Marlow is a good man and completely faithful to me. If there is any trouble between you, then you had better settle it yourself. The important thing is obedience and faithfulness. There is nothing that Marlow has done that makes me think he is not as good a man as I thought he was before."

" But he tried to make me fall," I cried in bewilderment. I could not understand what Jem could have to say in Marlow's defence. Murder was murder!

" I must hear what Marlow's got to say about that," Jem replied coldly. " But you've got to learn to rely upon yourself. If a man is trying to murder you then you have to kill him first." And with these chilling words he walked back to the cavern and disappeared inside. I could hardly believe that he was suggesting I should kill Marlow and yet what else could I understand from what he had said? I had no wish to kill Marlow, even if I had the opportunity, or anyone else for that matter. I should have thought that the important thing in our present situation was unity; no quarrelling but complete unity and confidence in one another. Did Jem think otherwise? Did he think that there were more important things than a spirit of comradeship?

He never encouraged us to talk freely to one another. There was nothing that bound us all together except the fact that we had all been attacked by the enemy and were all determined to fight against him. But there was no warm friendliness between us. With Jem himself I was aware of a warmth, a kind of love almost; but with the others? I realised that so far from liking them I found them strange, cold, and almost inhuman. Jack White had been so changed by the loss of his memory that the friendly, peace-loving boxer was now irritable, slavishly obedient, smouldering like a peat fire. The only person for whom I had anything approaching love, I realised, was Mr. Bowler. And he was dangerous to our cause.

But once the idea had been put into my mind, it was like a seed in fertile ground. I thought that if I could not kill Marlow myself I would stir up friction between him and Jack White.

I lay on the sand in the sun, thinking and resting. Occasionally my body would tremble as though I were in a fever. This was simply the effect of nerves.

And what was the point, I thought, of this collecting of stones and throwing them into the sea? How did that help us? Before long, I thought, Jem would be setting us to dig holes in the sand and then fill them in again. Perhaps he was pleased to think of anything that would keep us occupied. Perhaps he even thought that it would stop us from thinking altogether. It was quite clear that neither Red, Henry nor Marlow thought the picking up of stones and the cliff climbing were useless occupations. It was enough for them that Jem had given the order. They believed him. They were without memories. About Jack White I could not be quite so sure. He had not had the same time to settle down. It was possible that he would become as fervent a supporter of Jem's tactics as any of us. But he might not. For the moment he was docile.

You can't make a man do completely useless things without causing him the greatest unhappiness. It was the pointlessness of our activities that began to depress me.

It was almost frightening to realise that since Marlow had tried to kill me on the rock face, I had grown much more critical of Jem. It had not really occurred to me to question his methods before. And I was honest enough to realise that this was largely due to my resentment that he had done nothing, and apparently intended to do nothing, about Marlow. I thought that was personal treachery. Although Jem was not aware of it, he lost one small part of my allegiance at that moment. At the same time, of course, he lost none of Marlow's and perhaps that was more important for him.

This led directly to my first act of rebellion.

I made up my mind to find where they had put Mr. Bowler and what they had done to him. I realised that it was useless to go in search of him in daytime but made up my mind that I would go on a journey of discovery as soon

as everybody was asleep. I came to this decision immediately. The rest of the afternoon and evening then dragged very slowly by. Marlow seemed to be watching me with a triumphant grin on his face, and I made a point of keeping as far away from him as possible. Jack White was silent as always. Only Red and Henry talked together in low tones. Jem himself sat in the mouth of the cave with his back towards us, gazing out to sea.

We had made a fire of driftwood inside the small entrance cave; this was partly for warmth and partly for cooking purposes. A current of air was constantly moving in from the mouth of the cave and carrying the smoke off up the corridors that bore away into the rock. Otherwise we should have been choked out. It seemed that Red was the person entrusted with the job of feeding Mr. Bowler. He had made a sort of soup, for all of us, out of tinned meat, and potatoes; Mr. Bowler's share was taken away in a large tin mug.

Just who, I thought, were the crew of that boat? Where had they come from? And wondering over this problem which could not be solved without the help of Jem himself (and I dared not ask him), the slow hours before bedtime passed away. Jem, Jack White and myself slept in the same room that we had first been shown into. Jem occupied the camp bed. I was so much taken up by my plans that I only listened with half an ear to what was being said; ate my soup mechanically; could not join in the songs that Jem insisted on our singing. My fear was that I should be unable to keep awake when once I had settled down in my blankets. I had grown quite accustomed to sleeping on the floor. I listened to the shallow breathing of Jem—it was so shallow that I could not tell whether he was asleep or awake —and the gentle snoring of Jack White. And the drip of water near at hand from the moist rock. I struggled with my sleep as a man will struggle with a powerful enemy and all at once I found myself on the very lip of the cliff, fighting for my life with Marlow. He had his thick, powerful arms around me, his grinning face was close to mine and he was forcing me back, back, over the edge. He had clamped my arms to my side and I was powerless in his grip. Then I was over, falling and turning, seabirds whirling and crying around me, beating my face with the tips of their wings; and the sea and shore whirling up.

I awoke suddenly, snatched out of my dream by my fear. Perhaps I had cried out. I listened to make sure that my two room mates had not been disturbed but the black boxer was snoring heavily now and even Jem was breathing deeply and regularly. I was still wearing my clothes—indeed, all the time that I was in the cave I slept in my clothes, only removing them for the morning swim. I made my way out into the passage and, listening to the high whining of the wind in the sounding chamber of the cliff, made my way down to the entrance cave. Hurricane lamps were, as always, burning. The tide was in, calm and gentle, with the moon polishing its smooth surface.

Red had taken the extreme right-hand passage with Mr. Bowler's food. I knew that Red, Henry and Marlow slept somewhere up the central passage. Wondering what excuse I should make if caught, I took the right-hand passage and, immediately, heard the unsteady music of Mr. Bowler's sole companion, his whistle.

At the same time I turned a corner and stepped into impenetrable blackness. I called his name softly, for the whistling seemed close at hand. But it continued, uncertainly, wonderingly, like an April blackbird who does not know whether warm days have come to stay or whether the wind is going to swing round once more and bring the snow. Then a courageous trill to show that he has confidence in the blue sky and the thin sunshine; if he is not absolutely sure, he thinks that it is cowardly not to rejoice. And Mr. Bowler, somewhere in this blackness, behind I knew not what formidable door, chained to the wall perhaps, was playing to himself as though once more he were in the field of daisies and me a strange-faced boy peering over the stone wall to look at him. "Eh, what's all this, I'd like to know. Don't you like music or what?" I thought he would demand as soon as he knew that I had come.

I advanced cautiously, sliding my feet over the smooth rock floor. "Mr. Bowler," I said more loudly.

The whistling stopped immediately. I had come to what seemed a wooden door let into the solid rock. This then was his prison. I could think of no appropriate words to say.

"Hallo, young man," said the friendly voice from behind the door. "I had been wondering when you would come and see me."

"I hope you're all right."

"It's very dark."

"Is there anything you want?"

A pause. "Well, yes, there is. But I've always been wanting things, so it doesn't signify much. I shall always go on wanting. I shall always be dissatisfied. It's my character. However, I won't say that they overfeed me. And it's very dark."

"I'm very sorry." I pressed up against the door which seemed to be held in place by a wooden beam.

"And how are things going with you?" he asked, as though we had met casually on an afternoon walk.

"Things are going very well." I felt ashamed to tell him of the adventure on the cliff. I did not want to say that I was beginning to doubt the purpose of our preparations.

"I suppose the big offensive'll be starting soon," he said. If it had not been so impossible, I would have taken the noise that followed to be a sort of chuckle.

"Very soon," I said confidently with my mouth almost against the woodwork, for I was afraid of being surprised by Jem or, worse still, Marlow. "Things are going very well. We'll be starting almost any day now. Then you will be let out. It is only for a short while."

Mr. Bowler gave a melancholy sort of chuckle. "They will never let me out. Never. I'm not their sort and they know it. And neither are you, young man. If you don't know it now, you will."

"I have never been more sure of anything," I said firmly, "than just the opposite. I am one of them. I belong to them. How can you say such a thing?"

" You're a silly little fool," said Mr. Bowler. Instead of making me angry, this only seemed to add to my gloom. It was quite out of the question now to confide in Mr. Bowler my puzzlement over the picking up of the stones, the apparent lack of preparations for the coming struggle. But I would have liked to know his opinion.

" What do you do to pass the time? " I asked.

Instead of answering, he gave a little trill on his whistle.

While we had been talking I had been leaning against the wooden beam. Accidentally I had lifted it and to my astonishment I found that it raised out of the sockets. In a moment I had lifted it clear and pushed the door open.

" I have been waiting for you to do that," said Mr. Bowler simply, " though I wouldn't have dreamed of suggesting it. I thought I'd like you to think of it yourself."

The cave in which he had been locked yawned like a black pit in front of me and I was aware of Mr. Bowler only by the warmth of his breath on my face and his hand which suddenly came out, touched my face and then settled on my shoulder. I suppose that being in the dark for so long, his eyes had more or less got used to the dark.

" Where are the others? "

" Sleeping."

" Gang of criminals," he said scornfully and set off down the passage, stepping silently, holding me by the hand. When we turned the corner and stepped into the light of the hurricane lamp I had a great shock. Mr. Bowler had suddenly swung round on me and I saw that he was wearing a beard, quite a sizeable brown beard, which was a fair measure of the time he had been imprisoned. I had lost count of the days. He was, of course, still wearing his bowler hat.

I was now terrified by what I had done. What would Jem say? There was no doubt that I had broken one of his strictest laws, obedience, and I could not imagine what sort of punishment would be given to me for such a criminal act as letting a prisoner escape. If I could have made him go back to his prison, I should have done so. I even tried to find words to persuade him that this would be the best for everyone but he kept saying very quietly, " Poor boy, poor boy," sadly and rhythmically while he stroked my head. This infuriated me. I broke away from him.

" So you're not coming," he said.

" Of course not." I thought of shouting to awaken the others but feared what they would say when they knew I had allowed the prisoner to escape. By lifting the beam I had committed myself. But I would not go with him.

It was late, much later than I had thought. From where we were standing and talking I could see the entrance to the cave; the patch of light which had previously been silvery grey with moonlight and sea-sheen was now pale green. The dawn was breaking.

Then Mr. Bowler did exactly what he had done at the fair when the crowd had started to wreck the boxing booth. He suddenly bent down, gripped me round the thighs and threw me over his shoulder; it all happened so suddenly, that he was off towards the entrance to the cave before I knew what was happening. I began to shout at the top of my voice and hammer at his back. I suppose he had not counted on my resisting so violently; quite obviously it had spoiled his chances of a getaway. My shouts had aroused

the others and there was a sound of answering shouts and boots rattling over rocky floors.

Mr. Bowler dropped me like a sack of potatoes and bolted out on to the beach. In a moment, Jem was at my side. He was shoeless. The others pressed after him.

" What's the matter? " he rapped.

" That way—he's gone! " I cried and Jem with Henry and Marlow on his heels were after the runaway. Jack White was such a heavy sleeper that he had not been awakened. Mr. Bowler had no chance of course. They caught him before he arrived at the foot of the cliff path, I learned later. When they carried him into the cave he was limp like a dead man and there was a line of blood running down from a gash over the right eye. Marlow and

Henry took him back to the cell. By now, Red had come slowly into the lamplight, yawning and stretching, inquiring mildly what all the fuss was about.

I lay on the floor where Mr. Bowler had thrown me. Jem, his feet astride, stood in front of me. But what he said to me I did not rightly understand. The glimpse I had had of Mr. Bowler's chalky face and the dribble of blood disfiguring it shook me badly. Jem's voice went on quietly without any great emphasis but I was not listening. Between his legs I could see the light thinning; a grey sea was rising and falling under a pale green sky; but veins of red, like the graining of walnut wood, suddenly showed where the high, thin morning clouds were lying; the ridged sand outside the cave was suddenly netted with purple shadows, high-lighted with gold. Although I was not listening to Jem's words, they were cutting into my very flesh. But I could feel nothing. My nerves were numb and paralysed. Mr. Bowler's blood, the sign of first brutal violence, had shocked me. The trill of his whistle came back to me as a painful memory; and I gazed at the ripening day, the growing brightness of the waters, as though I could escape from the horror of the deed of murder, for I did not doubt that Mr. Bowler was dead, by counting the rise and fall of waves or following the flight of the seabirds who were already skimming the water.

" I'm proud of you," said Jem.

I looked up at him in astonishment.

" If it had not been for you, he would have got away. It was very brave of you. He is a dangerous man."

" But I let him out." I did not want to avoid anything of my punishment.

" I understand that. That was weakness. The affection you have for an old friend. But you grew out of your weakness. You realised your duty. You tried to stop him. That is the important thing. We can forget anything else."

I looked at him joyfully, hardly believing my ears. He was standing with his back to the entrance of the cave; his figure was outlined in gold and he looked larger than human; colossal, like a statue.

"That is something else which we must learn," he went on gently. "We must learn not to like people—that is, not to like individuals. Because individuals can play us false." There was so much intensity in his voice that I felt sure he was thinking not so much of the affection I had shown for Mr. Bowler as the affection I am sure he had for me himself. I wanted to say that I should never play him false whatever happened but the words stuck in my throat, as though the blood of Mr. Bowler had congealed there. I knew that I could not think of Jem in the same way as before.

Then he left me.

They all left me.

I lay on the sand and watched the sunlight creep across the opening of the cave. I saw the sea change from grey to olive green and then merge into a heavy oceanic blue. The tide was going out and the damp sand gave off a rich salty tang. Seabirds rose and fell on the waves. The long clear line of the horizon grew lighter and merged with the paleness of the sky so that there was no telling where the sea ended and the sky began. The shadows on the sand grew smaller and had almost disappeared. The sun was rising in the sky. Day was coming. Before now we had normally taken our swim. But to-day was different. To-day, great things had happened. I felt overcome with a sense of guilt. I had betrayed the trust that Jem had put in me; and then I had been responsible for the death of Mr. Bowler.

I felt that I had to choose between them, Mr. Bowler or Jem. They could not both be right. A breeze lifted some sand and threw it in my face.

I could not get the thought of Mr. Bowler out of my mind.

CHAPTER VII

I DESERT

JACK WHITE now began to worry Jem. This was plain to be seen. The negro could not understand why we were spending our time picking up stones and climbing cliffs when there was real work to be done. It seemed that the negro had developed a very real hatred of the police, the men who had robbed him and us of our memories, and was impatient of Jem's methods.

" The time is not yet ripe," said Jem shortly. " You must leave me to decide. The picking up of pebbles and the cliff-climbing are very important. You don't have to bother your head about what is going to be done. You just do as you're told and wait and see."

The negro muttered to himself. Our clothes were beginning to wear out and Jack White's jersey, in particular, was developing great holes. He was sensitive about his appearance. We had no means of repairing our clothes, no needle and thread even, but Jack White tried to weave the edges of the holes together by the fine wiry stems of some wild plants growing on the gentler slopes of the cliff.

As the negro continued to mutter to himself, Marlow intervened violently. " Keep your mouth shut, nigger, and do as you're told. Thank your lucky stars you're still alive."

There was a sort of feline spite behind the words. Jack White glanced up, for he was lying on the sand, and for the moment I thought that he was going to throw himself on the little man. Marlow looked as defiant and provocative as always. But Jem laughed and pushed him away.

"Perhaps I should say this." It was evening once more and we were sitting outside the cave on the sand which was still warm from the sun. "Don't forget that we are men the enemy has already attacked. Get that? By some means or other he has managed to attack each and every one of us. You must think his plan is a pretty poor one if all his victims are like us. We know. We fight. We resist. Understand? How do we know that he doesn't want us to attempt to fight him? If he can monkey about with our minds to take away our memories, can't he also put motives and ideas there at his own wish?" He looked round at us. "The answer is that we don't quite know. It is a thought that has been haunting me. Perhaps that by acting in this way we are doing the very thing that the enemy wants. We must be patient and wait. We must find out more. We must spy out the land."

"And the ship?" I asked.

"That has nothing to do with it." Jem swung round on me in such a heat of anger that I was startled. "Because we have certain friends helping us, we mustn't think that the going will be easy. The less you say about the ship, the better. Put it out of your mind. I wish I'd got some of this memory-destroying stuff," he added in a lighter tone.

There was no doubt about it. Jem was very sensitive about this ship. Perhaps he wanted us to think that the fight was being led by him when perhaps there were other and more important directors in another part of the country or, perhaps, across the sea. It was no new thing—Jem's vanity, and I put it down to this. If we had not known about the ship, our respect for Jem's organising ability would have been much greater. It would have seemed that he had performed miracles. But now it occurred to me that the reason for our delay was very simple. Jem was only a minor commander after all and perhaps we were waiting for the arrival of another ship with the man who would really lead us against the police. Lead us against the police? Wasn't the idea, after all, rather absurd? What chance did we few stand against a force of men, all properly organised? Undoubtedly, the leader we were waiting for would bring reinforcements with him. He would bring weapons and ammunition. Then possibly we should have to take a back seat. We were the advance guard. Possibly that is why Jem was so sensitive about questions on the ship.

Yet, at the same time, I could not see him showing any impatience. If we were waiting for the ship it would be natural for him to spend time gazing out to sea. At night it would be expected that he spent hours waiting for the orange light. But Jem slept as soundly as any of us and the sea itself might not have existed but for the morning swim.

I could not think about the problem as clearly as I should have liked because I was haunted by the thought of Mr. Bowler. Jem had not spoken of him since I had seen the old fellow carried in with blood on his face, and his silence seemed a sign that he didn't want the subject raised. But I had to speak.

" I want to know," I said perhaps in a bolder, more defiant tone than was really justified, " what has happened to Mr. Bowler."

Jem looked at me with a faint smile on his lips. " What does it matter what has happened to him? "

" I want to know."

"This is very touching," said Jem with a faint sneer, "this thought for an old friend. Very touching and affectionate."

"I want to know," I insisted.

"And then this thirst for knowledge!" He looked at me thoughtfully. "Come on."

He led the way up the corridor that led to Mr. Bowler's prison and I hesitated before following. I had a dread of his opening that wooden door and showing me my friend lying dead on the ground. In fact that is what I thought Jem intended. It would have amused him. But having asked my question I could not refuse to know the answer. I followed. We came to the corner where the light from the hurricane lamp was of no more use to us. Jem took me by the hand. "Listen!"

There is no describing my relief and joy. All the doubts and half-suspicions that I had been nursing were washed away. For quite confidently I could hear the trill of the tin whistle and I knew that Mr. Bowler was, so far from being dead, alive and sufficiently well to play. By this one stroke Jem had restored all my faith in him. He could tell me anything now and I would believe him. If he said that we should have to wait in the cave for a month, for a year, before striking—I should have accepted it quite cheerfully. I even began to make excuses for the rough way Mr. Bowler had been handled. I did not absolutely know, for example, but that he had received the blow on the head accidentally. Perhaps he had attempted to climb the cliff path, had slipped and fallen. In any case, the swing over of my feelings was from one extreme to the other. If I had been doubtful before now I was blindly faithful.

It was unfortunate for Jem that something should have happened immediately that destroyed all this faith in him as

116

certainly as if I had seen horns sprouting from his forehead, and the cloven feet of the devil himself planted on the rocky floor.

There was the pad, pad of feet behind us.

" Who's that? " demanded Jem. The both of us returned the way we had come. In the light of the hurricane lamp we saw Jack White approaching. " What do you want? " demanded Jem.

" I would like to have a word with you, sir," he said and with a shock I realised that the very quality of his voice had changed back to that of the Jack White who had told us the story of his life as we walked along the road from the fair.

" What d'you mean? Want a word with me? " Jem advanced towards him, blocking out the negro from my view, designedly I thought.

" You are a man of blood," said the negro quietly. " I can feel it. You are a man of violence and death."

" Don't be a fool. You're mad. What are you doing in this part of the cave anyway? Who gave you permission to follow us? "

" I gave that permission to myself. I ask permission neither of you nor of any man."

I could have cried out with joy. This, coming on top of the revelation that Mr. Bowler was indeed alive, was almost too much for me. Jack White was recovering his memory. This man talking to us in the cave was no longer the sullen, complaining negro who had tackled Jem about our in-activity. This was the old peace-loving negro who had allowed Jem to beat him in the fight so as to find a means of breaking his contract with the unscrupulous promoter. I tried to push past Jem in order to seize White by the hand. But Jem pushed me back.

" I understand," he said. Then turning to me. " Get out on to the beach and join the others. Quick! "

I dearly wanted to stay but realised that if Jack White were in the process of recovering his memory he must have the most careful treatment. I went out and sat with the others. Jem took Jack White off up the central passage, the one leading to the sleeping quarters of Red, Henry and Marlow; also the place where the stores were kept. And I excitedly told the others of the good news. They looked at me incredulously. Marlow alone seemed to resent the suggestion that there was a possibility of one of our number recovering his memory. But for the others, I could see, it was the greatest news they had heard for some time. Red's eyes glistened. He stroked his beard and wanted to follow Jem and White into the interior of the cave but I explained that even I had been sent back. Henry gave nervous twitches with his hands. If this were true then there was hope for all of us. If the enemy could fail in one case he could fail in them all.

Then Jem walked out of the cave and asked us what all the excitement was about.

" How is he? " I asked. We were all hanging on his words.

" He's asleep," said Jem curtly and would not allow the question to be discussed any further. Jack White, as it happened, did not wake until the following day. When he did he showed himself to be as truculent as ever; and any glimmerings of remembrance that he might have had were completely gone. I was bitterly disappointed. Perhaps I had read too much into the few words that the negro had uttered, even wondering whether I had imagined them. But no, the thrill that they had sent through me was un-forgettable. The negro boxer really had shown himself to be the peace-loving man of a few short weeks ago. But it had been merely a film that had passed over his mind, like a mantling of ripples on the face of a pool when the wind blows, only to disappear when the wind drops.

As soon as we were alone Jem asked me angrily what I meant by telling the others what the negro had said. I looked at him, dumbfounded; and then, as though realising his mistake, he turned on his heel and marched into the cave leaving me to look at the sea. So Jem had not wanted the others to know that one of our number had almost recovered his memory. He had been angry with me for what I had said. Why? I could not imagine. Surely it was the most wonderful thing that could happen. And even as I thought about it I drifted into one of those periods of Not-Knowing, when even the ground on which I stood did not seem solid.

I see things either black or white. There is no moderation in me. As soon as I realised that Jem did not wish us to recover our memories (and his anger could mean nothing short of this) then I thought of what Mr. Bowler had said. "You, you are the enemy," he had said. And Jem had had him locked up. Jack White himself had called Jem a man of blood. And Jem had taken him into a remote part of the cave from which the negro only emerged as half-witted as before. I say "half-witted" because in comparison with the mild boxer who had told us about chicken farming this is what he certainly was. What had Jem done to him in the innermost recesses of the cave?

Evening. The air and the sea were still, but inside me there was a storm. I was almost impatient with the weather for not blowing up a gale, for the waves to thunder up on the beach, for heavy clouds to fly across the sky. It would have been more in keeping with my mood. I doubted everything and everyone. Jem was a monster. I could believe nothing else. He had done something to Jack White to drive away the return of his memory. Why? The only explanation lay in what Mr. Bowler had seen long ago. Jem was the enemy. He was the person planning all the devilry of which he had spoken. If the police were so dangerous why had they done nothing more to us? Why were we allowed to live here in the cave undisturbed? The only explanation was that the police were innocent of our existence.

At that moment Marlow came stumping out of the cave, and gave me a sour look. " He says that you've got to look snappy and come on in." Then without another word he returned. After a few paces he stopped. " And get a move on," he shouted back. His voice went echoing away into the cliff. Then I could hear him marching along one of the corridors.

I think it was the way he took it for granted that I should do what I was told that angered me particularly. If Jem sent one of the others, Red or Henry for example, it is quite possible that I would have taken my orders more calmly. In that case events would have turned out quite differently for coming on top of my mood of terrible doubt the words irritated me beyond all measure. Why should I go back? Why should I do what I was told? I thought, and I suddenly found that I had risen to my feet and was hurrying along the beach to the point where the cliff path began. I say " I found myself " doing these things, because I did not so much make up my mind to run away, as have it forced upon me as though by some outside power. I did not know enough, I was not sure enough to take things into my own hands. If I had thought I should have realised that I did not know where to go or what to do. But I did not think. I was furiously angry. And I found myself wildly scrambling up

the cliff path in the evening light thinking of Mr. Bowler who had also made an attempt to get away and had been brought back with a wound in his head.

I had climbed half-way before I allowed myself to stop and look back. The beach was still deserted. From this point I could not see the mouth of the cave but that meant, at least, that anyone emerging could not see me. A great oily sea seemed to be swelling in towards the shore. The sun was on the point of setting.

Then, even as I looked down, I saw a figure come running out to the edge of the sea, so eager to gaze up that I saw the waves were breaking round his feet. It was Jem. I recognised him not so much by any details as by his whole familiar bearing, the angular way his arms seemed to be joined to his shoulders, the way he spread his legs apart. His shout came up to me and he was waving his arms wildly.

The boom of the surf made it impossible for me to hear what he said but it was not necessary for me to hear the words. I knew what he was crying but it was too late. I could not, for the life of me, have descended that path once more. There was no reason. But I felt impelled away from the cave as surely as if there were a magnet over the edge of the cliff top drawing me on. Before I turned to continue my climb I saw that Jem had been joined by others, Jack White and Marlow it seemed to me. They would be after me. I turned and scrambled at the rock with my fingers in an effort to get to the top as quickly as possible. I wanted to hurl myself into the green country beyond, conceal myself in some wood, hide behind a stone wall—anywhere away from the cave so that I could sit and think. My anger was already evaporating. My course of action had been decided. I was afraid of being caught. The hunt was on.

I was gasping painfully for breath by the time the dark evening landscape lay under my eyes. One glance back and downwards and I suddenly thought that it would be no difficult thing for me to stand at the top of the path and have my pursuers at a disadvantage. A disadvantage for what? There would only be sense in my staying there if I could hurl them to the beach below. But it was not in my mind to do any harm to them. If I were to cut straight across the field I knew that I should come to the cross-roads where we had seen the police notice posted on the stunted oak tree. That was the obvious way to take and therefore it was not the best way. I should have been wiser to follow the edge of the cliff for a while but I was so driven by my instincts that I did the obvious. I made for the stunted oak tree, making the chase much easier for my pursuers. I could not see the tree because the darkness now had become very heavy. Only when I looked round was there a sort of luminosity at the edge of the cliff; climbing up out of the blackness I saw the unmistakable form of Marlow—and behind him, Jack White. I knew that they could not see me. But they came running across the field in my direction and I did not wait to see more. The ragged branches of the oak tree loomed up in front. I clambered over the stile and immediately felt my side caught in a stitch. The pain was so sharp that I could hardly straighten my body. I knew that I could not continue to run in this condition and it would be necessary for me to hide. But where? Such hiding places as there were I thought very obvious. But the darkness was my friend.

I stood on top of the wall and from there found it easy to climb into the branches of the oak tree. It was late enough in the year for the foliage to be thick and unless my pursuers climbed up into the tree after me they would not know where I was. At about fifteen feet from the ground I wedged myself into a fork and waited. By leaning towards my side the stitch did not pain so acutely.

Almost immediately it seemed Marlow and the negro were at the stile, panting like great dogs. Marlow was in a particularly bad mood and was swearing under his breath. Nevertheless he was anxious to show that he was in charge of operations.

"You take that road, nigger," he said. "And I'll go this way. Remember as long as we stop him it don't much matter about anything else. We needn't bother about bringing him back."

It seemed that I could have reached down and touched the tops of their heads. Yes, it was an opportunity for Marlow to get rid of me and no questions asked. But when they set off my thought was not so much of fear as a strange sadness that the gentle Jack White should have been changed by this filthy drug, Jem's filthy drug I was now quite convinced, into this dangerous man-hunter. He would give me no mercy if he were to catch me. But I could not bring myself to think any harm of him. He was a victim. I was a victim. But Marlow, I thought, I should cheerfully have pushed over the cliff.

CHAPTER VIII

I MEET AN EMPEROR

WHEN I awoke it was still dark but there were bars of grey in the eastern sky. As soon as I attempted to move the most excruciating pains shot through my limbs. Held in one position for hours it was the greatest torture to attempt to move and it was as much as I could do to avoid crying out as I gradually levered myself out of the fork which had held me so securely. Like a stiff old man I slowly climbed down on to the wall. When I attempted to stand on my own feet I almost fell. I was so much occupied with the painful stiffness of my body that I did not give a thought to Marlow or White who were no doubt still in the neighbourhood. I was ravenously hungry.

I worked my arms and legs, gently at first, and then as the blood began to flow more freely through the limbs I did so with more energy. Fortunately the night had been warm for a light breeze had been blowing from the south. But my clothes were wet with dew and my shoes creaked when I started to walk. At every moment the light was growing brighter. At every moment I was feeling more and more hungry. And at every moment I was realising the stupidity of continuing along the road where I was quite likely to meet one of my pursuers. The first larks were singing, the morning was rustling like an immense silk garment, the polished grasses were gleaming in the first red light and in spite of the fact that I had no clear plan in my head, in spite of the fact that I should almost certainly be caught and dragged back to Jem at the best, killed by Marlow or injured by Jack White at the worst, it was impossible not to rejoice. I was free and my own master. I slipped over a stone wall at the side of the road and struck off cross-country, nevertheless taking care to keep close against another stone wall.

Away to my right was a sort of hollow. There was a small tightly packed little wood at the bottom and I hoped that it would also contain a farm-house but there was no smoke or other sign of the presence of human beings. The sun had sprung up and the hollow was filled with radiance. In whatever direction I looked there was no sign of human beings. But immediately, above the singing of the larks and the breathing of the wind I heard a sound like sighing. I looked round me. It was a very regular sound as though it were not a human being but perhaps a mechanical doll that was so afflicted. I came to the conclusion that the sound was coming from the other side of the wall. It was about six feet high at this point and I could only look over by digging my toes in and climbing up.

On the other side there was an old man with a grey beard mowing grass. He had his back to me and was swinging a scythe rhythmically, the steel winking as it caught the sun. I dropped down into the field on his side.

" Have you got anything to eat? " I asked bluntly. I was so hungry that I could think of almost nothing else. But the old man appeared not to have heard me for he went on scything with great deliberation, allowing a sort of moan of pleasure to break from his lips now and again. I walked round in front of him so that he could not avoid seeing me and asked him once more if he had anything to eat as I was starving. He must be deaf I thought. Then suddenly he saw my shadow on the grass in front of him, for the sun was well up now, and he almost dropped his scythe in alarm. Two splendid grey eyes regarded me from under bushy eyebrows. For the moment there was the greatest fright written on his face. He looked at me carefully, appeared satisfied, and went on with his work. The scythe sliced dangerously near my foot.

"Food! Food!" I shouted, pointing to my mouth and making chewing motions with my jaw.

"I suppose it must be," the old man said at last in a thin voice and looking up at the sun. He puckered up his face impatiently when I continued to shout and gesticulate. I was so furious with him that I even went to the length of laying my hand on the scythe. A look of terror immediately came into the old man's face. He made strange gasping noises and gripped the handle all the firmer so that for a time, although I did not wish to take it from him, I found myself struggling with him for its possession. He must have thought I was a thief after what was probably a very valued possession. But what made me release the scythe was the sight I suddenly caught of a khaki haversack lying at the foot of the wall. In a moment I was on it. Just as I thought. The old man's breakfast, bread, cheese and a bottle of still warm tea. I ate ravenously, tearing off chunks of bread and stuffing them into my mouth. Then cheese. I glanced up at the old man who was leaning on his scythe and watching me with a puzzled look on his face. I smiled at him feeling better already. I suppose that my stay in the cave had not improved my manners and the old fellow must have thought me some sort of wild beast. He could be a dangerous enemy with that weapon in his hand, it

occurred to me. If he slashed out he could have cut my head off. But my thought was nonsense. Enemies and friends, for us and against us! That was the way I thought now. It was the influence of Jem who had given me the idea of a terrible struggle that was going on. So that when you looked at a man your thought was, is he for me or against me. When the chances were that he was either quite indifferent to you or was quite ready to help you. This old man, for example, he was not protesting because I was eating his breakfast. I was the savage, the fellow who had tried to steal his scythe, but he was treating me as no enemy.

Then I felt ashamed. I had eaten all his cheese, three-quarters of his bread, and drunk a considerable part of the tea; and in all probability he was just as hungry as me.

I rose to my feet. Out of the corner of my eye I noticed

a spot of poppy-red suddenly appear in the corner of the field; but I did not pay it much attention as I was much too interested in the gleam that had come into the old man's eye. He had come to some decision and his hands were tightening on the scythe. I thought he was going to attack me. He was wearing a sort of apron round his middle much like the kind worn by carpenters, and from the large front pocket he produced a grey tongue of stone about nine inches long, stood the scythe on its wooden handle and began to sharpen the blade with short fierce strokes. I stepped back a pace.

"Oliver," a voice boomed. The old man shivered and stopped sharpening his scythe. His eyes remained fixed on me. I turned to see who it was. It was a woman. She was larger and rounder and redder in the face than any woman I had ever seen. You could not say that her cheeks were like apples. They were more like those crimson-skinned red cheeses you sometimes see. But she had very beautiful hair. She wore no hat and the great custardy-yellow mass was piled on top of her head. And she was brilliantly clad in a scarlet gown that swept the grasses. On her upper lip was the beginnings of a moustache. She stood between us and the sun and we were cast in shadow.

The old man suddenly dropped his scythe and took to his heels. In a moment the terrible woman was upon him and had gripped him by the back of his collar. "Oi, come here." She had a voice like a man.

She lifted him up like a dog and brought him back to the area he had cleared. "What d'you mean by it?" she suddenly shouted and peered down into his face. "Who gave you permission to come out into the field with that thing?" She still had him by the collar and shook him from time to time. He looked quite terrified. The red woman never took her eyes from his face but when I took a step back, meaning to climb over the wall, she called out to me to stop. "Don't you move," she threatened. There was a menacing vibration in the voice.

Then the great woman changed amazingly. She released the prisoner and was actually smiling. She showed two rows of even white teeth and brushed back her custard coloured curls with her left hand. Her cheeks were round and shiny.

"My husband," she said simply, and even her voice was changed. There was a cooing softness about it. She smiled at the old man and I realised that this was her husband. "My husband has very strange habits, you know. Especially since our son ran away from us. When I think of the men we employ it does seem rather foolish that he should come out here in this way and do all their work for them. Still, it was always his way. He likes to keep in touch with every detail of our estate."

She suddenly caught hold of her husband by the scruff of his neck once more as he had been moving towards the scythe which was lying on the ground. "Come far?" she asked me. "I haven't seen you about these parts before. On holiday?"

"I've lost my memory," I said, "and I've been living in a cave with some men who are planning to get control of the country."

"Nonsense," she said. "You've been reading too many books. How would you like a job on the farm?"

"I've lost my memory. I don't know who I am. And the country is in danger."

"You're mad. If you don't know who you are why don't you find out?" she snapped.

"And I'm being chased by two men."

" Serve you right."

" Why did your son run away? " I was furious that she thought I was lying.

She looked at me thoughtfully for a moment. " That is none of your business."

" When did he disappear? Down in the caves there are men who have lost their memories. What sort of a boy was he? Perhaps he is there. Perhaps I know him."

" He was not a boy. He was a man, very tall, very broad, strong, fair-haired like me. What you say is nonsense. My son would never live in a cave. He has gone to the city. He always said he would go to the city. As for you you're nothing better than a liar."

I was convinced that the woman was insane. She said that she did not care if her son did not come back. By running away he had deeply offended her. She would never forgive him. He would have been forty next birthday.

" If a man of forty can't leave home——" I was beginning.

" Turn him off our land, Oliver," she demanded loudly. " Chase the vandal off." The man pounced on the scythe with a quickness of action surprising in such an old man and turned on me, the terrible weapon in his hands, his eyes glittering.

" Vandal! Vandal! " the woman boomed. I was off like a hare, racing down the side of the wall, not daring to make an attempt to scale it for that would have given the old man an opportunity to catch up with me. But before I reached the end of the meadow I heard the great braying voice of the woman calling her husband off. From the security of the roadway I turned and saw the two of them, looking at something in the grass. Then the woman appeared to lift him up by the collar of his jacket.

131

By now the sun was well up. I had, at least, breakfasted, but the encounter had given me a sort of horror. They were the first human beings I had made since striking out on my own and I thought it a bad sign that they should have been insane. They would not listen to my story for a minute and had chased me away. In comparison with this pointless, selfish lunacy, the method of life in the cave seemed rational and much to be desired. But, having eaten, I was much more cheerful.

Suddenly my arms were seized from behind and I heard Marlow's unpleasant voice in my ear, felt his hot breath on my cheek, " Got you, you little swine! You dirty little——" and with each word lifted my arms, which he had pinioned behind my back, higher and higher, so that I cried out from pain. He could just rest his chin on my shoulder and when the agony from my arms caused me to twist my head on one side he immediately bit my ear. My idiocy in being so careless caused me almost as much pain as he could inflict upon me.

" Now, march! " he said viciously and began to push me along the road. There was nothing for it. He had me in such a grip that it was impossible to resist. To make matters worse I saw Jack White appear from over a wall. I cursed the bareness of the countryside that gave one so little cover.

" No, I can manage him," Marlow snapped as the negro came up. It was perfectly true. It was quite impossible for me to break away from that grip. " Stand off, nigger, I can manage him, I tell you. I could manage the little swine with one finger." He was pushing me along the road, jerking my arms so high that the pain made me feel sick. I was determined not to give him the satisfaction of hearing me cry out.

"Nigger, nigger," I heard the little man chanting with satisfaction. "I told you I'd get him." There was so much venom in Marlow's character that it had to out; either by torturing me or by insulting White. The only person to whom he was completely faithful was Jem. This in itself was a sign that Jem's cause was rotten.

Jack White suddenly roared and rushed upon us. For a moment I thought that, demented as he was, he meant to throttle me. But he gave Marlow a terrific blow on the side of the head which made him release one of my arms. Though he hung on firmly enough to the other. The black boxer's face was twisted with fury. Possibly he was jealous that Marlow had been the person to catch me, possibly the little man's taunts had at last become too much for him, but the beast in him was out.

Marlow's face went as white as paper. Over his left cheek-bone a line of red, as though drawn with a mapping pen, appeared, broadened and soon washed down the whole cheek. Still he held my wrist like a vice. It was only for a moment that he was dazed. Jack White withdrew a little uncertainly after he had struck the blow and in that moment Marlow pulled an ugly sheath knife from beneath his jacket where undoubtedly he had worn it on a belt. He was quick but I was quicker. His arm went back over his shoulder and I realised that he could have spitted the negro as he liked; but I threw myself upon him with all my weight, grabbing up with my free hand. I did not know what had happened to the knife. I felt Marlow's foul breath in my face and heard his scream of disappointed rage; then he was biting at my face. But Jack White was upon us. He caught Marlow by the throat and I suddenly found that I was free, free but almost blinded with blood that was running down from a cut on my brow.

It was a heaven-sent opportunity. I tried to smear the blood away with my fingers so I don't know what sort of grinning mask I had, but I was off down the road feeling like a hare that has escaped the hounds because they were at each other's throats to decide whose was the titbit. Escape? But I had not escaped. I glanced back and saw that Marlow was on the ground; he was on all fours and his head was hanging down almost touching the roadway. Jack White was after me. Whatever bad blood there might be between Marlow and the boxer, I was the important prize and it made me almost sick to realise that this was not so much due to any personal wish of Jack White; I was the valued prize simply because it would please Jem. I had a start of about fifty yards.

I could not hope to get away. I might have saved my energy, I well knew, for the negro was gaining on me with every step. I could hear him pounding along the road after me—and it was impossible for me to leave the road. It was beginning to descend here and banks were rising steeply on either side. At the top of the banks—which even at a time like that I noticed were bright with wild flowers—there were the inevitable grey walls. It was a straight run. There was no dodging. Nothing.

My heart seemed to have swollen to about four times its normal size and was thudding at the walls of my chest. The blood was flowing down my face more freely than ever. And with a shout Jack White was upon me. As far as I could judge without turning round he was no more than a pace behind and was, even at that moment, stretching out his hand to grab my shoulder.

Almost without stopping in my run I bent and flung myself at his legs with all the weight of my body. He was taken completely by surprise, right off his balance, gave me

134

a terrific kick in the side that hurt for days after, but fell
with all the force of his fourteen or so stone on to the side
of his head and lay in the middle of the roadway motionless.

It happened so quickly that I hardly realised what I had
done. Some instinct of self-preservation had told me what
to do and now my first thought was not that of flight but
that of concern for the man who, by devilry, had been
changed into my enemy. I thought for a moment that he
was dead. I was horrified. He lay on his back, his knees
drawn up, snoring as though it were three o'clock in the
morning and I still thought he was dead. It was some
moments before I could pull myself together sufficiently
to realise that a dead man cannot snore; the snoring itself
was so odd, so out of place, so uncanny. The area round
his left eyebrow was raw like meat, clotted with blood

which, for some reason, was not flowing. His face looked as though it had been torn by some wild beast. The unhuman snoring kept pace with the throbbing in my side. I realised that it would be madness to attempt to bring him back to consciousness. He would still be the demented creature that he was before the fall. I owed it to myself, and to Jack White too, to get away from the scene as quickly as possible. I must get help from somewhere. That help would release Jack White from the prison that he was in because I regarded the negro as being as much a prisoner as Mr. Bowler shut up in his cave. White was tough. I was sure that no serious harm had been done. He was even showing signs of coming round for the snoring had given way to moaning and his fingers were opening and closing as though he were searching for some better hold on the throat of an enemy. The only danger to him was if Marlow came along, saw him lying there and decided to finish him off with that knife.

Blood was seeping in through the corners of my mouth, salty and unpleasant. I began to feel faint. If I collapsed there I should have no hope of ever getting away; almost groaning with pain I climbed the embankment and with a great effort managed to climb over the stone wall where I found myself lying in sweet meadow grass.

It was too much for me. Although I fully realised the danger of my position I lay there feeling that the hard earth beneath me was the softest bed I had ever laid upon. The grasses seemed enormous forests. Ridiculously enough I found myself engrossed in watching ants busy penetrating what to them must have been a great jungle; they were scaling smooth trunks hundreds of feet high for no better purpose than to come down again; others were making their way across crazy bridges, wavering, thin blades of grass; and they ran over my fingers and I had not enough energy to brush them off.

I lay there in a daze for what seemed hours. The ants were walking in and out of an unpleasant dream and I had to struggle hard to realise that the small creatures I saw everywhere amongst the grasses were not part of my hallucination. The hum of insects oppressed me like the throb of great motors; the whole earth, it seemed, was vibrating, the sky itself shaking, and deep down inside me there was a vein that had been opened and was slowly draining my life blood away.

The sun was hot on my face. The blood had caked into a stiff mask so that it hurt me to make any sort of grimace. But I was pulling myself together; I was realising that by some miracle I had not been followed over the stone wall, I had been left alone to rest and recuperate my strength, and if only—ah, that was the great thing, if only I could have a drink I should be ready to carry on. But to get on to my feet! I lived through hours of effort and pain, it seemed, in order to draw myself upright with the help of the wall against which I had been lying. I knew now that I should have to look over the wall; and of all things this one act daunted me. I feared what I should see on the other side. I could hear no sound but the hum of insects. The wall was so low that I could look over without clambering up.

There was not a soul in sight. Tall daisies on the opposite bank seemed to be nodding their approval of what I had done; of Jack White there was not a sign. But in the middle of the road where he had been lying there was a patch of brown on the chalky dust. In spite of my weak state I wanted to cry out with joy and I don't know whether it was because my way to escape now seemed clear or whether it was because I now knew that the negro had got over his fall. Certainly I did not wish any harm to come to him— even though I feared him in his present state.

My first necessity was water. My tongue seemed to have swollen so much that it filled my mouth; and in addition to that I wanted to wash off the blood from my face. But it was a dry sort of countryside. There were few trees and the earth seemed bone dry, no rivers, no streams; and then I thought of the hollow I had noticed earlier in the morning before meeting the man scything and his mad wife. It had contained a small wood and was the most likely place to find water; failing that the mad woman's farm must be somewhere near. I might be able to obtain water without attracting her attention.

I kept close to the wall and following two sides of a triangle eventually arrived at the point from which I could look down on the little wood. There was no sound of scything coming from the other side of the stone wall so I supposed that the woman had taken her husband home. On the other hand there was not a human being in sight and I should have been glad of a helping hand. My side where Jack White had kicked me was aching abominably. As I made my way down the side of the hill into this pleasant valley so shut off from the rest of the world it seemed that I caught sight of something flashing among the trees. I screwed up my eyes but could make nothing out except the foliage of the trees which were, now that I was sufficiently near to see properly, magnificent beeches. I now felt so faint that I sat down on the grass. I plucked some of the long grasses and put them into my mouth, rolling them into a ball with my tongue but I found the taste too sickly and spat the green ball out on to the ground.

The shade of the trees looked very inviting. And then,

which made me rise to my feet and hurry impetuously on,
I saw unmistakable blue smoke rising through the foliage
and faintly blending with the sky. A cottage at least, I
thought joyfully, and hurried as best I could up to the edge
of the copse. There was a fence of barbed wire, but that
was not much obstacle for me. But once I had set foot in
the shade a small figure shot up from the long grasses and
dashed away calling out like a tropical monkey. His sudden
appearance gave me such a shock that I felt sick. It was a
boy, of course, three or four years younger than myself; his
hair, which was about as much as I could see of him, was long
and untidy. I closed my eyes and tried hard to think of
rivers and water meads, cool bubbling brooks, anything
which might have some steadying influence on a person who
felt that he was going to be sick. There was a great deal of
shouting going on amongst the trees, the high-pitched
squealings of the boy I had startled (or who had startled me
rather) and a deeper man's voice.

I stood as erect as I could manage and marched straight forward towards the voices. There was only time for the merest glimpse round when I came to a sort of clearing in the middle of the small wood. I saw two brightly painted caravans, yellow red and blue in the sunshine with a striped canvas awning rigged up between them. Underneath the awning in the cool shade there were people stirring, probably children and women-folk, but it was difficult to see clearly, for in contrast with the bright sunshine the shaded portion was quite black. But as I said there was not time for much. A man whom I took to be the very Emperor of the Gipsies advanced towards me.

For an Emperor he was dressed quite simply I thought. He wore brown corduroy trousers and a stained white shirt. He had tied a red kerchief around his head. But I knew that he was the supreme potentate of all the gipsies by his commanding size (he must have been at least six feet three in height and broad in proportion) and the truly extraordinary ugliness of his face. The various features of his face, his nose, his eyes, his ears, his mouth gave you this odd idea; that they had been placed together with no special reference to one another. They might have been taken from four other people and grafted on to him. He had a large bulk of nose, a pair of very small black eyes set as close together as his nose would permit, and one ear that stood out at right angles like a sail while the other lay flat against the side of his head as though in constant fear of being cut off.

" Who the devil are you? " he asked. He spoke fiercely out of the corner of his mouth and I think this was the moment when I noticed that he had a luxuriant bush of hair growing out of either ear. " No, it's all right," he grumbled. " It'll be all lies anyway." He lifted up his hand and would not allow me to speak. "Now—git!" He nodded his head and jerked his thumb.

With my face daubed with dried blood and my clothes torn I suppose I must have presented an odd sight; but this reception bewildered me. It bewildered and angered me.

"Give me some water. Can't you see I'm hurt?"

The gipsy breathed fiercely down his nostrils and stretching out one hand seized me by my jersey. "If you don't clear off before I lose my temper I'll turn your head round on your shoulders."

Immediately a small wiry woman with wisps of grey hair across her bony face flew out from the shelter of the awning and caught hold of the gipsy by the back of his shirt. "Charley," she ordered. "Loose go of him at once."

There was silence. There was not the flutter of movement. Everyone might have been turned to painted stone. "Loose him," the woman repeated and the gipsy's face began to twist up into what I suppose was meant to be a grin.

"That's all right, Meg," he murmured. "I was just questioning him. Can't be too careful . . ."

"Loose him! That's better. There are times when I get sick of you. Go on! Farther off! What if it is a trap? We'll give him a proper welcome. Then it's up to them to start the nasty business. Nobody can blame us, see?"

The grey-haired woman had taken full charge of the situation. "Now, who are you and what do you want? Lord protect us, it really *is* blood." She caught me by the shoulder and peered into my face. There was concern in her eyes. "Come over here and sit down."

I could not understand why I had been received with so much suspicion but at least the woman seemed well disposed towards me now. I followed her over to the caravans where she clapped her hands and shooed at the people under the awnings. There were two more men, not half so formidable as Charley, and a girl sitting there out of the sun busy with basket work, but at our approach they got to their feet and took their work round to the shady side of one of the caravans. I stretched myself luxuriously in the shade, lying on my back, but the woman said that she was going to have none of that and I had better stir myself at once. Or there would be trouble. I found a pan of water under my nose. Thinking it was to drink I put it to my lips but she stopped me, sent for a mug and gave me a drink. Then I was told to wash myself.

" Are you from the police? " she asked me directly when I had finished.

" No, I think I should like to find them." I felt fine now. I felt cleansed inwardly and outwardly.

The woman got to her feet, mumbling. I heard her talking to Charley, shaking her head. " Can't be, can't be. We can't live like this. We shall be going out of our minds." And then turning to me, " What's your name and where do you come from? "

I did not know what to answer. I realised that my story sounded so wild and improbable that it would only cause the gipsies to suspect me all the more. They noticed my hesitation. Charley swung away from his wife. " It's some damned trick, take my word for it."

" How can it be a trick? Can't you see that I've been attacked? All I wanted was a little water and now I can go on." I attempted to get to my feet.

" Who are you? " repeated Charley. The woman was watching me with her arms crossed.

" My name is Roger. I've just escaped from a gang of

men who have been holding me prisoner in a cave in the cliffs."

"Where?" asked Charley. He did not seem to be at all surprised by the information I gave him, so I told him and his wife quite fully what had happened. I told them that I felt quite helpless and could only imagine that I must get to the nearest town as soon as possible and put myself in the hands of the police.

"The police!" Charley laughed scornfully. "That gang of cut-throats. I reckon those men who held you in the cliff were police all right. Know why we suspect you? We think you've been sent here to spy out the land. What harm are we gipsies doing? Well, you can at least get back to your precious police and tell them that everything is above board with us."

I had so much made up my mind that everything Jem stood for was evil and everything he had told me was lies that when I heard the gipsy say that the police were nothing but a gang of cut-throats and that he suspected them of being the men who had held me captive, it seemed that I had dropped into a bottomless pit. Was there nothing I could know for certain? I felt the hostility of Charley and his wife as they stood in front of me and did not doubt for one moment that what they told me was true, the police were criminals. Did then that prove that Jem was right? Did it mean that I had been acting in a foolish way? And was the best thing I could do to go back to the cave in the cliff and ask for pardon.

"What do you mean?" I asked.

"You say that you've lost your memory," Charley said. "Then you don't know that the police force is organising a great wave of crime in this part of the country." He looked at me. I found his ugliness not unattractive.

"I had been told that," I answered—"but, oh it's so complicated. I don't know what to believe. I don't think the police are doing anything of the sort. I think you are mistaken." And what else could I believe? It would have injured my pride to go back to Jem and admit that I was wrong. Therefore my pride told me that I was right. That the police were good honest fellows, that Jem was a villain and these gipsies mistaken.

"I'm going to the police," I said.

"You've been well treated by us," the woman put in sharply. "You've got nothing to grumble about remember." I felt ashamed of myself to think that she still suspected me of being a sort of spy. But right or wrong I had determined to make my way to the town and give myself up. I was sick of this uncertainty. I wanted to know. So thanking the gipsies for their kindness and saying that they must believe me, that what I had said was perfectly true, I left their little clearing and found a lane to which they had directed me.

But I had covered no more than a hundred yards of the lane perhaps before I heard a shout behind me. It was Charley. He was following me and calling on me to stop. When he came up I could see that he had tidied himself up, put on a clean shirt, removed the kerchief from his head and tied it loosely round his throat. On his head was a wide-brimmed straw hat.

"I'm coming with you," he grumbled. "Yours is a strange yarn. If you're a liar then I'm going to protest to the police. I'm tired of their dirty ways. It's my right to protest. I shall get everybody to protest. And if what you say is true—then it's just a human action to come with you and see you dealt with fairly."

I was overjoyed.

After an hour's walking we came to a wide saucer of country with holts of beeches standing round the rim. I saw that the golden weathercock was flashing in the afternoon sun on top of the church spire which was clearly to be picked out as a lovely finger of cheesy yellow stone. The blossom had gone from the fruit orchards.

Before entering the town Charley produced some sandwiches from his pocket and we sat on a bank to eat them.

PART THREE

CHAPTER IX

OUR FEARS CONFIRMED

THE LAST time I had visited the little market town it had been dark and I had not seen very much of it. Although I looked out for it the fair had, of course, moved on by now. But the town itself delighted me. All the houses were made out of the local grey stone, but it was not the cold greyness of the walls that divided up the country. There was a warmth about it, a touch of gold, as though the sun, by shining on it for centuries, had seeped into the very heart of it. And everywhere were green orchards, at the backs of the houses, dividing them, and then folding the whole town round like a shawl. It was the time between the blossom and the harvest. I could see small green fruit like pebbles on the trees.

The town was grouped round a large square in the middle of which was a green and a war memorial; this was a stone cross rising from a plinth on which were carved many names. There were a number of shops, the Post Office and a square white-washed building with steps leading up to it, that Charley the gipsy told me was the police station.

There were not many people about and I remember looking at them curiously, a couple of boys sitting on the plinth of the war memorial, a woman crossing the green with her shopping basket, and a young woman gazing down from the upstairs window of one of the houses. They were normal, ordinary people. They knew who they were, had homes to go to, recognised their friends and relations when they saw them. Whereas I . . .

Inside the police station was a sergeant on duty. He was sitting at a desk with a telephone at his right hand. He was making entries in a tall, narrow book. As soon as he saw us he put his pen behind his ear and slowly straightened himself in his seat. He was a very young man to be a sergeant, I thought. He had a round, almost babyish face and a pair of pale blue eyes which were naturally apprehensive; but now he was looking suspicious.

I imagine that people did not normally visit his office except under protest; to see the gipsy and me walk in because quite obviously we wanted to be there he naturally found unusual. He was so much on his guard that he did not say a word, gave a glance at me and then stared at Charley.

" Who's in charge here? " demanded Charley.

" I've seen you before somewhere," said the sergeant.

" Are you in charge? " Quite obviously the sergeant was not used to being questioned in this way. He was so surprised that he was answering politely. " The Inspector is in there." And he nodded at a glass door. From the other side of this door we could hear voices, but although it seemed that the Inspector had visitors Charley had opened the door before the sergeant could protest and shown the Inspector quite clearly that he was going to receive more visitors. I am quite sure that the sergeant had been intimidated by his extraordinary ugliness.

When I entered the Inspector's office Charley was already in the middle of his speech. The Inspector, a man in a tunic that clipped him tightly round the throat, an elderly man with grey hair brushed straight back over his head, was looking at him almost red with rage.

" Get out! " he yelled. " Who in the name of hell allowed you in here? Get out."

The sergeant had seized Charley by the arm but the gipsy was quite capable of shaking him off. " You'll be sorry for this," Charley said, and then, " Let me go, damn you," to the sergeant. " This boy's got a mighty strange story to tell and if you'll take a tip from me you'll hear it now, on the dot."

" I take tips from no one. Get out."

I was very much impressed with the police station. It was the first real building I had entered since losing my memory, for you could hardly call the cabin on the hill a building. The smart uniforms, the bright buttons, the authoritative way the Inspector spoke, obviously a man used to being obeyed, all these things were a little too much for me. I wanted to tell Charley that we had better go outside and wait until we were called for. But Charley and the Inspector were doing so much shouting, Charley insisting on his right to be heard by the representative of law and order, the Inspector drumming nervously with his fingers on the desk and giving short barks of fury, that it was impossible to make myself heard.

Charley had tackled the Inspector immediately on entering his office, so I had not noticed the other person, the man to whom the Inspector had been talking. Now this man suddenly sprang up out of his chair and with a piercing cry succeeded in silencing even Charley.

" Now you're going to start are you? " asked the Inspector.

"I insist on people respecting my position. You forget that I represent the——"

"That's the boy," the man was shouting, pointing at me. "He's one of them." He came over, towered over me, bully that he was. "Where are the others? Where's that rascally, contract-breaking dope, that black rogue you spirited away with you? Where is he, eh? Where's Jack White?"

It was the boxing promoter, the man I had last seen waving bank notes in desperation while the crowd proceeded to break up his booth. It was a stroke of outrageously bad luck.

Even Charley fell silent. He looked at me uncertainly. I had not told him all the details of our exploits at the fair and there is no doubt that he was wondering whether there were a number of other disgraceful and compromising deeds that I was concealing.

"I thought I'd seen you afore," said the sergeant to Charley.

"Shut up. Close the door, sergeant."

"I was a fool to come, I suppose," said Charley gloomily.

The Inspector's rage had vanished. He was even smiling, looking comfortably from the boxing promoter to me and then over to where the gipsy was glowering in the corner. "There is obviously some deep laid scheme here and it is quite a fortunate chance that you"—to the promoter—"happened to be here. Now, no lies, did you or did you not enter this man's sideshow with the deliberate intent of inciting the crowd to smash the place up? And secondly, did you or did you not do so with the object of allowing the pugilist, Jack White, to escape, not only breaking his contract but also taking a considerable proportion of the evening's takings?"

"Jack White take the——" I could not believe that he had done anything of the sort. No, it was impossible. This was an invention of the boxing promoter.

"Then you admit to knowing the man White, you admit all this?"

"Yes, but . . ."

"That's quite enough. Put them in the cells sergeant."

"But he's got nothing to do with it," I protested as the sergeant tried to seize Charley. The Inspector coldly ignored my protest. He pressed a button on his desk and two constables appeared. If I was surprised by Charley's docility it was all explained to me in the cell when he threw himself on to the single bed that was provided and bemoaned his luck for having got himself mixed up with a lying rogue. He meant me. Once the police get their hands on you, he said, then it was all up. Useless to try to resist. Useless to protest. In fact all the spirit seemed to have gone out of him as soon as the door clanged behind us.

"It's not my world," he protested. "A gipsy in prison. It's not like an ordinary man in prison. I would rather they had flogged me."

"But I'm not a liar," I said, and tried to explain the truth. But the gipsy had seemingly made up his mind that it was too late for truth to matter. Whether what I said had any truth in it or not did not get us out of prison. When I said that they would have to give us a fair trial he laughed and said the police were not going to allow two promising convicts like us to escape as easily as all that. "Where are your witnesses, anyway?" That was true. I needed the presence of Mr. Bowler badly.

"All we have to do," said I hopefully, "is to explain to the police about Jem, the cave and all that. They will go there, arrest the whole gang and we shall be released. I shall be a valuable witness."

The gipsy sat on the bed looking at me. " I don't know why it is," he said slowly, " but in spite of everything I believe you. I think you're straight. But the world is a very difficult place for straight people especially when they are in clink."

I was so overjoyed that he had some confidence in me that I wanted to go over to him, make some demonstration of my gratitude, but there was a tenseness about him that checked me. He was talking in my presence and yet he was not talking to me. He was struggling with something inside himself—possibly he was wondering whether he had done right in coming with me to the town even though he was convinced that I had been telling the truth. Perhaps he was wondering whether there were times when it did not pay to tell the truth, support people who were honest, fight against the wicked. There was a struggle going on inside him and I felt that any word or gesture from me would be a sort of interference he would be impatient of. I kept silence.

" Don't worry, son," he said at last with a miraculous smile that illuminated his ugly face. " Don't worry. I've got an idea that we shan't be in here very long anyway."

" As soon as I tell them about Jem . . ."

" No, not that, son. I've an idea that the police wouldn't be particularly interested for the moment. They are too happy and pleased with themselves. Been doing a lot of business."

" Then what? " I asked.

" You've been telling me the truth, eh? Well then, it strikes me that this Jem of yours, if he knows what he's doing, will be acting on a pretty big scale very soon now. Then we shall get out."

I did not understand. " Better to be in the hands of the police than in his hands."

"We've got to wait and see. There's nothing we can do."

"But they must listen to us."

"Shout your head off—but they won't listen. Meg'll be furious. That's what's worrying me. You've no idea!"

The room in which we found ourselves was not a real cell. At least it was not what I imagined a real cell to be like. There were bars over the window and the wooden door had been strengthened with strips of metal nailed on to the woodwork; but it was an ordinary room converted. There was even wallpaper on the walls, covered with pink and blue flowers which, before long, I found myself counting in order to pass the time away.

It was a very small room. But the police had determined on treating us well, it seemed, for a second bed was shortly brought in; this left very little room for walking up and down, which I thought would be very necessary for exercise if we were going to be kept here for long. And I was not so optimistic as Charley. The police treated us well, gave us good food, because I suppose there was no earthly reason why they should treat us badly. I was now quite prepared to believe in Charley's statement that the police in this particular town made it their business to stir up trouble in order to justify their existence. All they wanted was crime and prisoners. To treat their prisoners badly did not enter into the scheme at all; it occurred to me that they might even treat their prisoners so well as to cause a certain amount of competition for the pleasure of being locked up.

Charley was magnificent. He said that he could not imagine any magistrate sentencing us. That is to say, he would not sentence us until my story about the cave had been thoroughly investigated; for Charley appeared to think that although the police force might be corrupt the magistrates were not.

Charley treated me on equal terms. I appreciated this enormously. Though there was no doubt of his own importance among the gipsies (my thinking he was the very emperor of the gipsies was not so very far wrong as I came to learn afterwards) he spoke to me as though I were his equal in age and importance. It was the very cleverest kind of flattery. Perhaps he thought I was in more need of cheering up than I actually was, but, whatever his reasons, I was very grateful for his trust in me.

And it turned out that he was quite right. Jem did not delay striking. That night we spent in the cell was the only one. The following morning we were released under the most extraordinary circumstances; released into a world where, although we had been locked between four walls, we had the feeling of coming out into a larger and more terrible prison. The spirit of Jem hung over the town like a pall and the gipsy Charley and myself were the only two people who had any real understanding of what had happened.

We slept well. In the morning we were awakened by the sound of shouting in the street but this noise soon died away and there was a heavy silence which Charley said was very unnatural in a town that was normally so very busy. Time went by. There appeared to be nobody stirring about the police station and eventually Charley and I fell to hammering on the door, hoping that at least somebody would bring us breakfast or water in which to wash. But our knocking echoed through the station as though the place was deserted.

Suddenly the door was flung open and we found the sergeant, the same one who had received us the afternoon before, looking at us stupidly. " What are you doing here? " he asked. He had not yet put his jacket on, was wearing shirt and trousers, and was carrying a cup of tea in his hand. " Who are you? " he asked.

He had the same innocent blue eyes, was still the same young-looking sergeant, but if he had shown some strange, lizard-like deformation, if he were an unpleasant freak, a two-headed man, if his skin were scaled like a fish, I could not have looked at him with more horror. I could not get out of the cell for he was standing in the doorway and although I realised that he would not attempt to stop me from passing, nevertheless I found it impossible to run the risk of touching him. I had the feeling that I was living through the experience for the second time. And it was true. Jack White, the black boxer, had behaved in much the same way after the first night in the cave.

"Do you mean to say you don't remember us?" Charley demanded.

The sergeant did not answer. He frowned as though trying to remember and then turned away. Charley did not wait for any more.

"Come on, lad. Now's our opportunity to make ourselves scarce." He pushed the sergeant aside and I followed him out in the passage, wondering whether we were going to meet any of the other constables. But there was not a soul. We opened the door and went into the sergeant's office and with a thrill of unpleasantness I realised that he was following closely on our heels, saying not a word. Charley was concerned with making sure that the coast was clear so that we could slip away but I found myself engrossed with the way a black cat was behaving itself. As we came into the office the cat lifted its head from a saucer of milk and looked at us strangely with a white, wet beard. Then, with a puzzled, confused air, it smelled the saucer, its own paws, neglected to wipe its beard and wandered vacantly round the office as though it had not seen the place before. It took it to be some strange place from which it was an important duty to escape. Finding the door it suddenly shot down the steps into the sunlight.

"Tell me," begged the sergeant, "what is happening. I've lost my memory. I don't know who I am." There was such a note of self-pity in his voice that, in a flash, he was no longer horrible. I could feel nothing but compassion for him. I desperately wanted to help him, but I knew from experience that there was very little I could do. I tried to tell him not to worry, to remain where he was for the time being, and, since this was his own town, doubtlessly somebody would be along shortly to look after him.

"Look at this," said Charley between his teeth. He called to me from the steps where he had already ventured. As he did not whisper I thought there was no longer need for caution and went out to join him.

What I saw was at once perfectly normal and yet perfectly frightening. Men, women and children, some of them not completely dressed, but wearing a dressing-gown or even a sheet thrown over their pyjamas and night clothes, were wandering about the streets as though the houses did not exist. They gave the illusion that they could not see like ordinary people for they were ignoring one another completely, not speaking, but gazing around them as though they had been miraculously transported to a South American forest. I recognised the emotions that were flowing through each of these individuals as though they were flames visibly running through their limbs. I recognised the doubt, the half fear, the timidity, the wish to make friends, the fear of being repulsed, the fear of being insulted, the ardent longing for somebody to take them by the hands and say, " I know who you are. There is no need to be afraid." I recognised the feeling for it had been my own when, on that lonely road, seemingly so very long ago, I had come to the realisation that I did not know who I was. On that occasion there had been Mr. Bowler with his whistle and his amazing calm. But there was nobody to comfort these people. Except myself. Oh no, but it was so much beyond me, I was so incapable of going out into the street, of making a speech and telling them that all would be well. What notice would they take of a boy? For there was no doubt that every man, woman and child in sight had, by some devilish stroke, been robbed of his memory that morning. How?

"You see," I said to Charley. "Now do you believe me?"

He was looking round in bewilderment. "The whole place has gone mad."

"Not mad. They don't know who they are."

I could not imagine how Jem, for there was no doubt in my mind that he was at the bottom of this, had succeeded on such a great scale and overnight. And as soon as I thought of Jem I realised that he must be somewhere very near. Even now he might be watching us. Even now Marlow or Jack White might be on their way to make sure that the beautiful pattern of his plan was not spoiled.

Two men, labourers of some sort by the look of them, began quarrelling at the foot of the steps. They were quarrelling not because they were angry about anything but because they feared one another. They could not trust one another. They suspected one another. As if every human being in sight were connected to the two men by invisible wires I could see the doubt, the suspicion, radiating outwards from the quarrelling pair. They suddenly grappled and fell to the ground. The crowd watched uneasily but no move was made to separate the two. Charley trotted down the steps and picked the two men from the ground, gripping them by the backs of their jackets, and shook them impatiently. "Fools, fools, idiots," he roared. "Aren't things bad enough without you scrapping?" He shouted at the top of his voice. "Get to your homes, everybody. Get there and stop there. And if you don't know which is your home get into somebody's house, wash, eat, keep yourselves warm. Above all do not quarrel." But they looked at him as though he were speaking a foreign language. I knew that numb, frozen feeling. Charley released the two men. One of them was bleeding from the mouth. They glared at one

another as though anything were preferable to Not-Knowing. Men just have to get in touch with one another. And having an enemy is preferable to having nothing at all. I could see that these two men were glad of their anger and resented the strength of Charley which had torn them apart.

Some of the people, the women especially, made a move towards the houses and I could see that there was going to be competition for the better houses. At once, on the other side of the war memorial, fighting broke out and there were eight or nine struggling figures on the grass. Fear ran through the people like a wind through corn. To my heated imagination they seemed to ripple physically. But what strange harvest was this? And who would be the reaper?

"We can do nothing for these people," said Charley. "Best thing is to get on to the phone with the next town."

But when we tried we found that the phone was not working, either because the wire had been cut or because the exchange workers were in the grip of Jem's poison.

The worst feature of all was the feeling of helplessness. It did not appear that a single inhabitant of the town had retained his memory, or at least they did not come forward. I could not imagine that Jem had succeeded in drugging every man, woman and child in the village. The exceptions no doubt would think that either the world had gone mad or that they themselves were mad. Unlike Charley and myself, these unfortunate creatures would be quite ignorant of the causes of the calamity; and perhaps from certain points of view it would have been better if they had suffered the loss of memory also. I could imagine them, locking themselves in their rooms, or trying to talk rationally to people who no longer recognised them although the night before they had been the nearest relations.

By now there was an atmosphere of panic in the town. The inhabitants were for all the world like a flock of sheep, alarmed at they knew not what.

"The fools," said Charley. "Look." From the upper windows of one of the houses facing the green a sudden belch of black smoke gave warning of a fire. A chair whirled through one of the windows but it was clear that this was not thrown out in order to preserve it. Inside that upper room fighting was going on. Charley ran down the steps of the police station calling on all the men in sight to give a hand in order to put the fire out. Quite a number followed. It was a natural thing to recognise that fire was an enemy. Even the loss of one's memory could not take away that instinct. Indeed, curiously enough, the work that was now necessary in order to put out the fire seemed to have a steadying influence on the crowd. The men on the green gave up fighting, the panic died down, and there was a calmness about the scene that made everything seem almost normal. Charley disappeared into the house, followed by a number of men. The window of a greengrocer's shop was smashed and a number of women could be seen helping themselves to the fruit. I looked around in despair. Even if Charley succeeded in putting out the fire I thought that not very much would be accomplished. We had to do something more radical in order to make sure that the population was not completely at the mercy of Jem and his gang when they arrived, as arrive they shortly would, on the scene. The only thing that could be done was to set out for the next town. Here, if the population still had their memories, help would be available, doctors, nurses, food, supplies. If the next town were in a similar state then one must not lose courage. It was impossible that Jem could have overwhelmed the whole country at one stroke. But in spite of my knowing what should be done I remained where I was. I had a feeling that in spite of all common sense my duty was here.

Then I saw what I had feared to see. I saw a man who remembered. He was an oldish man dressed in an old, stained brown suit. He came out of a side street and looked round him in complete bewilderment. He was too far away for me to hear what he was saying but I could see him going up to individuals and, quite obviously, addressing them by their names. But they looked at him with incomprehension, he shook his head sadly and continued his search for someone who would tell him that he had not gone mad. That person was me.

"My name is Roger," I said, thinking it best to tell him something quite simple and definite to begin with. "I expect you are puzzled by all this. It is really quite simple.

The town has been attacked by a gang of men who have made everybody forget who they are."

He looked at me not with amazement for it was quite clear that the sight of the town itself had sucked out of him all his capacity for being amazed. He would have listened to the most inconceivable story quite calmly. He was prepared for any horror. But I was not prepared for his next action. He raised his fist and struck me a blow on the face that laid me on my back. And then he walked off jerkily, looking anxiously into the faces of all he met. "Is the world mad?" he started to shout. "Oh God, what a hell is this?" The people looked at him as though he were a possible enemy.

The smoke belching from the house had considerably abated. Although my head was spinning from the blow that the man had given me I got to my feet and went over in search of Charley. I met him at the door. His face was smudged with black and his shirt torn from shoulder to waist. "The others—putting it out—they're good lads—know what to do." His chest was heaving. He took great gulps of the fresh morning air. "Who's that?" he asked, raising his hand. I turned and looked in the direction in which he was pointing, and saw a figure standing on the plinth of the war memorial, raising his hands as though to quieten a noisy crowd. But the people gathered in the square were silent. There was no mistaking the jaunty, confident air of that figure, his red hair, the bold way he tilted his head and looked around. It was Jem.

"That's him," I said. "That's the fellow."

Charley looked steadily at Jem. "And the others?"

Then I noticed that, posted all round the square, were men with revolvers in their hands. They were standing at the strategic positions, the point where the roads entered the square, the entrance to the little alleys, at the doors of the larger houses. I recognised Marlow and Jack White immediately. There were the others, too—Henry, for example, standing not twenty yards away but gazing so fixedly at Jem that he had not noticed me. Yes, Jem had seemingly brought off the capture of the town. He was beginning to talk, the undisputed master of the town and all its inhabitants.

"Listen to me everyone, everyone," he was shouting at the top of his voice. Such was the force of his personality that the crowd drew nearer. Where Charley and I had failed Jem was succeeding easily. He was making the crowd listen to him and I knew immediately that he would be able to persuade them to do just as he wished. Even the man who had not forgotten was standing at the foot of the plinth with his mouth open.

"You are all puzzled, you are all bewildered," Jem was shouting, "I understand. You must have confidence in me, you must listen or you will be lost. You must do as you are told. For your own good you must obey me." He spoke well and persuasively and although there were no smiles on the faces of any of the crowd the tenseness seemed to have gone out of them.

"I'm off," said Charley. "You be good now, that's all." And before I could protest he had disappeared into the house once more. And yet could I blame him? He had his family to think about. It was his duty to get back to them as quickly as possible and make a move to some other part of the country. Possibly I should be doing the best for myself by running away, too. Because I did not doubt that he would be making his escape by the back door. Nothing, however, would have persuaded me to act in this way. The very sight of Jem standing on the war memorial and making his lying speech infuriated me. I had to protest by

some means or other, I had to let them know that they were
being imposed upon by an arch-villain. But how?

The door of the next house was standing open as indeed
were the doors of all the houses round the green. But it was
not being guarded by anyone with a revolver. Moving
slowly so as not to attract a great deal of attention I eventually reached the door. No sooner there than I turned and
hurried up the stairs to one of the front bedrooms where I
threw the window open and looked down on the scene in
the square. Jem was still talking. The crowd was getting
thicker. He was getting a response from the crowd. They
were murmuring approval. Jem was telling them about the
wicked enemy that had taken their memories away and
explaining that their only chance lay in . . .

It was too much. I leaned out of the window and shouted

at the top of my voice. " He's a liar! It's lies! Don't listen
to him! Pull him down!" By the time I had finished shouting
there was a silence. Jem turned and looked up at me. He
shook his fist. At the same moment I heard the sharp crack
of revolvers and bullets shattered the glass of the window.
I darted back into the room realising when it was too late,
that I had acted in the most idiotic way imaginable.

Already there were footsteps on the stair.

CHAPTER X

THE BATTLE OF THE VILLAGE

I LOOKED hastily round the bedroom in which I found myself. It was very simply furnished, like thousands of other bedrooms I suppose; a single bed with the clothes thrown untidily back as though the sleeper had awakened in a panic, a wash-bowl, a small table with a mirror and a chest of drawers. But there was nothing that I could use as a weapon and I realised that the time had come when I could defend myself with nothing else but weapons. I could not talk to Jem with anything save something that would hurt him. But here there was nothing. Not even a poker. The room was a trap. I could see no way of escape.

I ran out on to the landing and found that, as in so many of the houses of this kind, there was a sky-light at the end of the landing so as to give light to what would otherwise be a very dark place. If I was going to escape then this was the only way. I darted back into the bedroom even as the foot-steps on the stairs seemed perilously close, picked up a chair and ran to the end of the passage where I placed it under the skylight. With its help I found that I could just touch the skylight with my head. To my joy I found that it was, as I had hoped, the kind that opened like a window, and it was only a moment's work to throw it back flat, though as I did so there was the sound of splintering glass. I will not say that I was frightened. I was gnawed with a terrible sort of anxiety, but there was no more fear in it than there would have been had I been running for the last train that would take me away from some remote place. This anxiety gave me power to swing myself. The chair went over with a clatter, one of my feet was flat against the wall; then, with a superhuman effort I levered myself through the opening and found myself standing in a little bay let into the steep slope of the red tiled roof.

At the same moment I realised that my pursuer had caught up with me. I looked back through the opening and found Jack White's ebony face upturned and shining with perspiration. There was an expression on his face not of hatred of me, as I might have imagined, but a sort of blank determination to do the job that he had been ordered to carry out. I don't know why but in looking down upon him my feeling was not so much of fear or even resentment but only of pity. He hardly knew what he was doing, but nevertheless I had to protect myself.

It was an easy matter to prise one of the tiles out of the roofing and this at least did provide me with some sort of weapon. As soon as his black hands came over the edge of the sky-light I brought the tile down upon them with all my force; there was a kind of high wail from inside the house and the hands rapidly disappeared. It was an impossible situation for me of course. I could not hold the negro at bay indefinitely and, for all I knew, there might be others already working round to get at me from some other quarter. But I stayed there waiting for the hands to reappear as I was sure they would. But it was his head that popped up and this was so little expected by me, for I had forgotten that he was so tall, that for the fraction of a second we just gazed into each other's eyes and the dead look on his face particularly struck me. I brought the tile down on his head with so much force that it broke in two and the fragments clattered after him as he went sprawling off his chair and crashed on to the floor of the passage. I felt like a criminal. I was so much horrified by what I had done, for I was quite sure that I had killed him, that I gave up my strong point and began clambering along the steep slope of the house top.

I realised that it would be suicidal for me to walk along the ridge of the roof for there it would be the easiest matter in the world for one of the gunmen below in the square to pick me off with his revolver. I had to remain where I was for the time being, using what protection the house gave me. The red tiling on the roof of the next house was of exactly the same colour as that of the house on which I found myself and because, from the position where I was, there appeared to be no gap between the houses, it will be understood how I thought that the roofs were continuous. It was a sort of optical illusion. I had made about three-quarters of the distance along the roof when I realised there must be a considerable space between the two houses. When I reached the end I found that this distance was about twenty feet and had it been a hundred feet my chances of jumping it would not have been less. I looked round.

The orchards were so thick that a green sea seemed to be swelling around the houses. Some of the trunks had been painted white. Beyond the orchards were other cottages and beyond them a blue road which leisurely wound away into the distance. What would I not have given to be safely on that road and I almost succeeded in convincing myself that I should be transported there simply by staring at it.

I looked back the way I had come and found the black
head of the boxer sticking through the sky-light. The shock
was not so great as it might have been for, to my surprise,
I found myself experiencing relief to know that the negro
was not, after all, dead. This was quite illogical for the
thickness of his skull meant that I was to be captured. He
came slowly out of the opening—I thought of it as some
monstrous birth that was taking place—and began to make
his way cautiously towards me.

There was nothing that I could do. I felt calm and
resigned.

"Jack," I said, for he was reasonably close now, "don't
you remember me?" He came on with a frown on his face.
Blood was running down from a wound in his scalp.

I could still hear the voice of Jem echoing shrilly on the other side of the square and the murmuring of the crowd which was like an inland sea. He was winning their approval. He was forcing himself upon them. There was nothing that could resist him. I had been a fool to think that I could escape and worse than a fool to imagine that I could fight against him.

"Jack," I said, "stop a minute and think. Don't you remember me?" I hardly knew what I was saying. I had enough reason to know that this same Jack White, the man who had hated violence so much that he could not kill chickens and had even given up boxing, had had another character foisted upon him by Jem. If I could only break through to that original Jack White—but all this was not so much thought as felt, passionately wished for, as it was my only hope.

"For the love of God stop a minute, Jack," I cried.

There may have been some quality in my voice, it may be that the height we were above the ground had caused him to be dizzy, it may simply be that the blow on the head affected him more than I had thought, but he came to a stop not ten feet away from me and regarded me with large puzzled eyes as though he had not seen me before.

"There is blood on your face," I said. I experienced a wild surge of hope. "It is running down from your head on both sides of your face."

"That is nothing," he said, not taking his eyes from mine. "Blood is good."

"Not your own blood, Jack. You are not your own enemy."

"Who is my enemy?" he asked calmly, still not moving forward.

It was amazing. I could hardly breathe. I felt as though I were watching some tight-rope walker a thousand feet in the air. He was turning and swaying. Would he fall and go crashing to the ground or would he regain his balance? I wanted to stretch out and give him some support.

"I am not your enemy, Jack. I am your friend. But you have an enemy."

"I must catch you. I have been told to catch you," he repeated solemnly. But I could have cried out with joy. I was breaking through, it seemed, layer after layer of deadening wrappings to an essential Jack that, if he was not the Jack White who had been on the point of recovering his memory in the cave, was at least showing himself to have some streaks of humanity. It was not now the time to wonder about it. It was possible that the terrific blow he had received on the head had caused some sort of brain disturbance. In any case I had nothing to lose and there was everything to gain by being bold. Instead of waiting for him to come up to me I crawled the ten feet of tiling until I was sitting at his side and put my hand on his shoulder.

"Why should you catch me? I am a boy, look! Why should you want to catch a boy?"

He made no answer but I could see that I was troubling him.

"I am not your enemy. I am your friend. You must believe me." Patiently and speaking with the greatest clearness as though he were deaf, I explained that Jem was the enemy, that he had robbed Jack White of his memory and was making him do senseless things. I told him about his previous life, about the chicken farm and the boxing.

" Chickens? " he said doubtfully.

Jem was still making his speech. The crowd was silent once more, listening intently I supposed. " That is our enemy," I said.

" I must take you to him," the negro said.

" Very well. You can take me to him and we shall see," I said. " But you must promise not to allow him to harm me. If he is not the enemy then he has nothing to fear. I am ready to go to him if you wish."

" I have been ordered to bring you to him," he murmured dully, as though trying to probe into the depths of his being. My heart sank for I had hoped to stir up his memory of his true self, but I realised that Jem's potion was too strong. At the most I could only hope to make him doubt. I could not make him believe me. Under the circumstances all I could do was to allow him to take me down to Jem. I could not escape. I had come to the end of my resources.

" I am sorry that I had to hit you with that tile," I said. He did not reply, so I went on. " You have a revolver. Why did you not shoot me? "

" I am told to bring you back, not kill you," he answered. " Come, we've had enough talking." With a touch of his old brutality he pushed me in the ribs and I led the way back across the roof to the sky-light. It did not now occur to me to make any attempt to escape. I felt that things had been taken out of my hands, that I had done as much as could really be expected of me. Now somebody else must do something.

A few minutes later the crowd was parting to allow the negro and myself to pass through. A silence had fallen upon them and Jem, I could see, was waiting for me with a smile of triumph on his face.

It was ironic that I should be brought as a prisoner to watch his triumph. This man whom I had believed in, this man for whom I had collected pebbles and climbed cliffs, this man, for whom I had deserted Mr. Bowler, was now the person I most hated in the world. I had not known what hate was. Looking at that smiling face I felt an uprising of so much emotion that I wondered at myself. It was an emotion so deep that it was deeper than reason, an instinctive loathing, such as we have for the more unpleasant reptiles. If the Devil himself were to appear, I imagined him to be something like Jem, smiling, calm, supremely confident of victory, exulting in his immediate triumph.

I found myself standing on the plinth at his side, looking down on the upturned faces of the townspeople. They believed passionately in what Jem had told them. Of that I was convinced. Now he would go on and extend his reign to other towns, counties, the whole country. But as I looked here and there in the crowd, there was doubt, uncertainty, by no means the unanimity I had feared. It was as though Jem had been drawing with a masterly hand on a surface of sand over which the water was constantly swilling, so that his work was washed away as soon as executed. There was still hope, I told myself. Everything depended on these people.

"I should be allowed to speak," I shouted at them angrily.

"Speak by all means," said Jem politely. He was so confident of himself. I turned and looked at the crowd. I felt a great longing inside me to help them. Although most of them were much older than myself they appeared to me as helpless children. I yearned to help them. For the first time I had the feeling of loving human beings. So much hate for Jem and so much love for the townspeople before me almost tore me in half. I wanted to utter some powerful word that would make them understand; but such a word I knew I could not find.

"Poor child," said a woman almost at my feet. Looking down I saw an elderly, plump woman who undoubtedly saw in me a child to pity. It had never occurred to me to be sorry for myself. I heard other women murmuring. The great thing was that Jem had not killed these things. He had not killed pity. So I began to talk to them with great confidence.

"I do not know what he has said but it's all lies. It is he who has——" but before I could go on Jem had grabbed me. I felt indignation sweep like a wave through the crowd. What had I done? What had I said? Then I realised that there was nothing but my own personal appearance to win me the sympathy of the crowd and Jem had realised too late that he had erred in allowing me to appear. He was much stronger than I. I struggled in his grasp. But both of us were suddenly folded round by a more powerful grasp and I heard Jack White's voice roaring in my ear. He had seized both of us, holding us crushed against one another. To this fact I undoubtedly owed my life for otherwise the gunmen posted on the outside of the crowd would have fired. They could not do so for fear of hitting Jem.

"He is a liar, a liar," I shouted, though the grasp was so powerful that I could barely get sufficient air into my lungs. Jem struggled furiously, screaming at the negro in rage.

I heard the crack of revolvers. The crowd was in movement. Hands were plucking at us but even as they were laid upon me I felt them snatched away by others. The crowd was fighting amongst itself and this could only mean that it had divided into two factions, those who believed what Jem had told them and those who had, for some reason or other, disbelieved him.

Extreme rage gave Jem strength. He was twisting like an eel, working his elbows into my side; but I had no breath to cry out. Jem suddenly had the idea of biting the negro's arm. I could see his head go forward and hear the cry that Jack gave out. The wound must have been deep for I immediately found that I was free and the negro had dealt Jem a blow that hurled him to the ground.

I looked at Jack White. Was he friend or foe? What was the explanation of his conduct? He was looking from Jem to me and then to the now struggling crowd. There was such an expression of awful doubt on his face that I realised that he was neither friend nor foe, that there was no explanation for what he had done, but some sort of instinct that had raised itself against Jem—why? that was something too deep to be thought about just now. The important thing was what he was going to do.

We were immediately attacked by a big red-faced man. The black boxer gave him one look, and then with the greatest hesitation, as though he hated what he was doing, knocked the man head over heels back into the crowd. Jem seemed to be gathering himself together. I cried out, but it was too late. He had thrown himself upon the boxer, urged by that wild bravery which had always been so characteristic of him. Surprised by the sudden onset, the negro lost his balance and fell over into the crowd, hugging Jem to him.

It would be a mistake to imagine that everybody was fighting. That was simply the impression that I had to begin with, but now I could see that by far the biggest part of the crowd that had been packed into the square was trying to get away. Only the tougher and more impetuous individuals were fighting, women as well as men. A cascade of water suddenly descended from one of the upper windows of the houses. Judging by the screams it must have been hot. At every doorway it seemed there were small groups striving to get inside. It was every man and every woman for herself. Even though I felt sure that Jem had lost control of the town for the time being and would find it extremely difficult to get it back again, he had done more harm to these people's minds than could be imagined. At my feet two wiry looking men were standing toe to toe and slogging into one another. There was a whine and a sudden spit of sound. A piece of the stone cross chipped off. For a moment I did not realise what had happened. Then I knew. Somebody had fired at me. I plunged down into the crowd and struggled to make my way to the side of Jack White, who, by now, had overcome Jem once more and was clasping him to his breast with his powerful arms.

"Over here," I cried. I wanted to get him and his prisoner out of the crowd and thought that the best place to go to would be the police station. I hardly dared to hope that Jack would follow but after a moment's hesitation I found him bearing after me. It was comparatively easy for me to work my way through the crowd, for I could dodge the struggling groups. But Jack White bore his way through them like some ship breasting through the waves.

And all at once it seemed that we were going to win. I hardly know what gave me thus sudden confidence, but I could have burst out singing. I was triumphant. I felt there

was nothing that I could not do; then I realised it was because of the way Jack White was doing what I had told him, because of the way he had seemingly given up his allegiance to Jem. This was, I knew, a very great victory.

I ran up the flight of steps and stood there waiting for Jack to reach me. The sergeant came out from his office and looked at me. Since I had seen him last, he had dressed himself properly and was looking as neat as when Charley and I had arrived the afternoon before.

"I am a policeman," he announced. "Get off these steps."

But I realised that he only knew he was a policeman because it was the natural deduction of a man dressed in blue who found himself living in a police station. This did not mean that his memory had been restored to him.

"We must get this man into a cell——" even as Jack came bearing up the steps with Jem in his arms I felt my right arm freeze. It was just as though it had been plunged into a barrel of ice and I looked down at my fingers in amazement to see the blood oozing round my fingernails. There was very little pain. My arm had gone dead. I had been shot in the arm and immediately took cover behind one of the pillars. The sergeant was automatically taking charge of the situation. He took one look at the boxer and his prisoner and ushered them through to the cells. A moment later I cautiously followed, wondering why I was feeling no pain in my arm, fearing to examine it closely, and yet feeling strangely proud of my injury.

I met the sergeant. "I've been shot in the arm." There was undoubtedly a pleased note in my voice. "Where are they?"

"In the cells. Where do you think? That's where you're going too."

I suddenly found that he was supporting me in his arms and the floor was heaving like a sea beneath my feet. Indeed, I might have been on some sort of boat for the crowd noises rippled, swelled and withdrew like the waves. The sergeant carried me through water, it seemed, water that descended from the walls of the police station and bubbled up gaily from the floor. There was no danger of drowning for the water, although it came up to our faces and covered our mouths, was light and gassy. We could breathe it in and out comfortably. Then I was back in the cave, walking up the dark corridor, looking for Mr. Bowler whom I feared was dead, only to hear his whistle shrilling away and feel the wooden door of his prison beneath my hands.

When I came to I found myself lying on a bed with the sergeant looking seriously down at me. My arm now ached abominably and by turning my head I could see it stretched out on the white sheet with a bandage tied tightly just above my elbow. It was this bandage that was causing all the pain. My arm was throbbing.

"What has happened?" I asked the policeman.

"You've been shot in the arm. But I can't do anything. The bullet is still there. You need a doctor. I've stopped the bleeding."

"Where are the others?"

"The fighting has stopped." The sergeant seemed well pleased with himself. I could hear shouting and banging coming from the corridor where the cells were located, and afterwards discovered that the sergeant had been filling them up during the course of the fighting. At a suitable moment he would dart down the steps and grab anybody he was sure of being able to overpower. In this way he had about

twenty prisoners and now they were shouting] to[be released.

" Who's won? " I asked.

" What do you mean, who's won? Nobody's won. They've been burning houses, smashing windows, robbing. What do you mean, who's won? "

His idea of the fighting was very different from mine. To him it must have been all a part of the strange dream he was living. He had no conception that one side might be right and the other side wrong.

" I want to see the black man," I said.

" That's what you think. I'm keeping the whole gang locked up and if it wasn't for your arm you'd be along in there with 'em."

" I must see the negro."

" Seems to me he started all the trouble. The other chap seemed to be quietening everybody down. Soon as you and the nigger arrived on the scene—oh yes, I keep my eyes open. I saw you. I know what's going on and it's no good pretending you didn't lay into that there chap. Well, whatever the rights and wrongs I've got 'em both locked up. We'll sort it out when we've got some proper order."

" Have you telephoned for help? "

The sergeant hesitated. " That's enough talking. Just lie quiet." He looked at me but apparently coming to the conclusion that I couldn't do much harm where I was he went out. In spite of my anxiety to get Jack White out of the cell, I could not blame the sergeant. In some ways I admired him. In all this chaos he had seized upon one important thing—the fact that, although he didn't quite realise why, he represented law and order. He meant to do his best to maintain it. He did not realise the uselessness of what he was doing, but duty was a sort of straw he clung to. It was clear that he had been unable to telephone for help. It would be an elementary precaution on Jem's part to cut the wires.

But the sergeant had been too optimistic about the end of the fighting. Although there was now a silence, a heavy silence hanging over the town, it was torn by the spiteful crack of a revolver. Then silence once more.

The sergeant came in. I asked him what had happened.

" They shot a man walking across the green."

" Let the black man out," I said.

" What did I tell you? " he shouted, though he was angry more because he did not know what to do than anything else.

"Those men are murderers. In a minute they will come in here and release Jem—he's the man you took with the negro. They will probably kill us."

"You're lying."

"You saw the man shot yourself."

He hesitated. "Darned if I know . . ." He went out. In his absence I counted the throbs of my arm and listened for the sound of more firing. None came. I could not understand why Marlow and the others were not coming to Jem's rescue. I could not believe that we had made the cover of the police station without being seen.

Then Jack White was standing over me, looking down with that dazed expression on his face as though he were staring into utter darkness.

" What you done to yourself? " he abruptly asked.

The sergeant was standing close behind to see what was going to happen. If any nonsense started there is no doubt that he would make a valiant attempt to put Jack back in the cell.

" Hurting, eh? " he grunted and there was a tenderness about him. In a moment he had slipped the tight bandage off, but this brought such an agony that I cried out. All the force of my blood stream was surging against a wall of fire in my arm.

" You fool. He'll bleed to death," cried the sergeant.

Jack White did not answer. The blank look had left his face, and he was looking down on me with the greatest concern, an expression that was worth all the pain that my body was capable of bearing.

" You must look out. Marlow and the others will be in." Even now the pain was slackening, and I was getting the use of my fingers. There was very little bleeding and Jack gave a grunt of what was nothing but pure pleasure.

" You remember me, Jack? You remember the boxing and the . . ."

" No, I don't remember you, lad. Except as something that . . ."

I felt that a battle was being fought here and now much more important than any battle with revolvers and fists. The fact that I was disabled spurred me on. If I could only win the negro over to my way of thinking, I do not think I should have minded falling into Jem's hands once more. I was struggling for the possession of Jack White's mind. If I won I felt that Jem would never win.

" Look," I said. The sheet at my side was stained with blood. I wanted him to look at it. But the sight of it seemed to cause him pain; and at that moment Marlow entered the room with a revolver in his fist, and told Jack White and the sergeant to put their hands in the air.

Just at the moment when I had thought success was in my reach I had failed once more.

CHAPTER XI

I AM A PRISONER

"MILK," SAID Jem in triumph. "All done with milk. But our methods are not going to be the same in every place. That is one of the secrets of the success that will be ours. In the next area of operations it will be easier to pollute the water supply."

Now that he was really in command of the town, Jem was seated behind the Inspector's desk quite ready to unbend and explain how it all had been done. I was lying on the floor. Although my injured arm had weakened me and made me not very much use for anything, my feet had been hobbled with handcuffs. Jack White was handcuffed and bound, lying in the other corner. Jem was having his lunch. It mainly consisted of roast chicken, which he ate with the help of his hands, glancing in a satisfied sort of way now at Jack White and now at me.

"It can't be done," I said, much more bravely than I felt. "The people from the next town will be upon you."

Jem gave a really sweet smile. "Your mind is uninstructed. I should have taken you in hand much earlier but now, I am afraid . . ." he waved a chicken leg in the air. "I was a fool to allow myself to like you. That is one thing to remember. Never like anybody too much. Never feel sorry for them."

"The people from the next town . . ."

" —will believe what I tell them," he shouted. "Do you think that I am a fool? Do you think my plans are not laid? If I could fool you and the nigger, I can fool anybody. I shall be the man to lead them against the monstrous enemy"—he laughed with his mouth full of chicken—"who fights with this terrible new weapon. Who is the enemy to be next time, eh, Marlow?" Marlow grinned and nodded his head.

"Next time I shall inform everybody that it is some foreign country. I will pretend to have such knowledge, so many secrets, and—they will trust us, won't they, Marlow?"

"You can't do it," I said.

"Meaning that you will tell them? And what makes you think you will be here to talk, you and the nigger? You, him, and Mr. Bowler—yes, you see, I still remember that gentleman, though I was a fool not to get rid of him before—we shall get you all nicely put away with no fuss. No sentiment. Before you die you will know that you have had the privilege of seeing a great man. You, an errand boy, and you a broken down boxer—and a tramp. Bowler and his red house in the park! A tramp, a tramp, I say," he shouted at me as though I had argued with him.

"What is my name?"

"I don't know. An errand boy, nothing, nobody. It doesn't matter who you are. The main thing is to get you both out of the way before we have any visitors in the town. I won't offer you anything to eat. Seems such a waste of food. If you were going to live . . ."

He stared at Jack White, who was looking at him fearlessly. "You are looking at a great man, nigger." He put the chicken back on the plate, got to his feet, walked over to where the boxer was lying.

"I hate the sight of you because you are my failure. I hate the sight of you both. You are the only people I've failed with. Just cussedness on your part, nigger." He stirred him with his foot, but Jack White did not even blink his eyes. "You could've been sitting on clover and your mind went click. Well, I don't like people who let me down. Got no time for 'em. And you had two doses of the stuff, that's the queer thing."

For a moment there was silence. "I hate the sight of blood," said the negro at last. "That was what upset me. It's deep inside me and you can't touch it. And I hate you."

"Thank God," I said in spite of myself. This confession was all that I could have hoped. It was coming to myself on the country road, and seeing Mr. Bowler sitting in a field of daisies. It was walking along a dark tunnel and hearing his whistle coming out of the darkness itself. It was plunging into the red morning wave. It was food after starvation, drink after thirst. It was sleep after work.

"Take them out and shoot them," said Jem, returning to his chicken. "What's the matter? Aren't you frightened?" He was looking at me. "You should be, you know. You're going to die."

Marlow was already helping Jack White to his feet.

"Yes, I am frightened," I heard myself saying.

"Good."

"But now I know that you can't succeed. Your filth isn't strong enough. It wasn't strong enough even for me. It wasn't strong enough for Jack White. And there will be many Jack Whites. They will not believe your lies. They will not be taken in with your talk of enemies. They will know that it is no foreign country. They will . . ."

187

"That is true. But you are being dealt with. We shall find ways of dealing with the others."

Now that the negro was on his feet he shook himself so violently that Marlow was thrown against the desk.

"I'm not going to have any rowdyism in here. Get a half a dozen men." Jack was too well secured to be of much trouble to them. As for myself, possibly because I was weak because of loss of blood, I felt a strange willingness to go. I was afraid, it was no good denying that, but I wanted to walk out of the office on my own feet. This I was not allowed to do.

Jack White could not walk, of course. It took four men to lift him and they did it with great difficulty for he was struggling as much as his bonds would permit.

I had confessed to Jem that I was afraid, but there was more in it than that. Even though I thought I was going to an immediate death, I still had a corner of my mind active to explore other ideas than the sudden bullet; I did not think only of my end. Jem had seemed so powerful, so irresistible. When I came to look back it seemed that I had never really hoped to defeat him. When I had heard him winning over the crowd there had been a voice deep down inside me that said, "Never, never, never. Nobody can stand against him." It was this feeling of helplessness that had been the worst part of the fight. And yet in spite of it I had been forced, by a power inside me, to continue. I could have made my escape at the same time as Charley the gipsy. But I had remained. I did not blame him for getting away.

But when I had sat on the sloping roof top with Jack White looking blankly at me, I had the feeling that the struggle might not be entirely hopeless. Jem's war was a war against people's minds, and if Jack White could resist him, in spite of having received a double dose of the drug, then there would be the greatest hope for all of us. Mr. Bowler had withstood it. I had withstood it after some hesitation. And now if Jack White, through anything I might tell him, could also win through to a disbelief in Jem, could remember just so much as would allow him to depend on himself and not on Jem, if my words would build up this confidence in himself without causing him the awful doubts that set one part of a man's mind at war with the other, then there would be nothing to regret in our deaths.

Oh, I know that Jack White and I would not be there to fight against Jem. But this was the way I looked at it. What I had done, what Jack White had done, others could easily do.

And because of this I was not so frightened of dying as I might have been.

But Jack White and I were destined to go through the door as free men. We were to walk out unfettered, not trussed like animals for the slaughter. Instead of our going out it was somebody who came in; and that person was Charley the gipsy. I looked at him unbelievingly. I could not understand what he was doing there. Why had he been such a fool as to come back and put himself into the hands of Jem? He was as ugly as ever, of course, but there was a radiant smile on his face that transformed it. Before he could speak, other blue-coated men had pushed past him into the room and Jem was going forward cheerfully to meet them. They were policemen.

"Indeed, I am very glad to see you," said Jem. "You've got here a bit before I expected but not too soon." He spoke to a policeman in a peaked cap, a sort of Inspector I should imagine.

"Is that the man?" said the Inspector to Charley.

Charley nodded.

"It's been like living in a nightmare," Jem went on blithely. "What these poor people need more than anything else is food and shelter. I fear that there have been a number of deaths."

"Why are these two tied up?" asked the Inspector.

"For safety. They're pretty desperate and the biggest liars you've ever come across. The nigger is a runaway boxer—he got away with the takings. The boy is a vicious criminal. They are the local agents of this gang, make no mistake. The stuff was planted in the milk supply."

"Set 'em loose," said the Inspector curtly. He took off his peaked cap and went over to the desk, where he sat down and looked at Jem long and hard. In a moment I was free, one of the policemen having handcuff keys in his pocket. I said that I should like to see a doctor as my arm had gone numb again, and I feared some sort of infection might have been set up.

"But you can't do this," cried Jem impatiently. "These two are the cause of the whole trouble. If they are treated in the right way we shall find out just what country is behind it all."

"What country?" said the Inspector coldly.

"Sure, this is a big thing, an international thing."

"All right, Sam, you can take him." Before Jem could move handcuffs were snapped over his wrist and he was looking incredulously at the Inspector.

"But don't you believe me? This is . . ."

"We're going to believe this fellow for the time being." The Inspector nodded at Charley. "This is a very strange mix-up, but I've a pretty good idea that we've got hold of the right person."

I was just beginning to realise that I was not going to be shot. The relief was so great that I knew I had been making a superhuman effort to control myself previously. I felt now as though my backbone had been removed.

" No, he's the chap and no mistake," said Charley. " Saw him with me own eyes preaching away there. Heard about him from this lad. In any case there'll be enough of his gunmen to be rounded up. That'll prove any sort of case against him."

Jem seemed to be getting smaller, to be shrinking into himself. His bluff had not come off and now he knew that he was beaten. The arrival of the authorities from the next town had taken him completely by surprise. Charley had gone for help, not made for the encampment as I had thought. So that Jem had been lost, his cause vain, right from the beginning and all that I had struggled for, all my fret, need never have been.

I felt at the same time elated and cast down. It was the greatest thing that Jem was now safely a prisoner but when I thought that I should have acted more sensibly by getting away with Charley I felt a fool. I had been a fool. There was no doubt about it. In my pride I had thought I could make some sort of speech and sway the crowd against Jem. That had not happened. Some old women had been sorry for me, Jem's treatment of me had caused resentment, and because everybody was in a very excited state, they had begun fighting. They would have fought about anything, I thought bitterly, food, a handkerchief, but not because Jem was a liar and their enemy. I suppose the weak state I was in due to the wound made me feel more unhappy than would normally have been the case. I looked at Jem once more.

He was holding himself stiffly erect and looking at the Inspector almost with contempt. There was a certain amount of fighting going on in the streets and occasionally the sound of a revolver shot would be heard. The police were rounding up Jem's gang. Suddenly the cat I had seen first thing that morning jumped on to the Inspector's desk and began washing itself. Everybody in the room looked at the cat. It also had drunk milk and forgotten. Being an animal it did not seem to matter so much. It did not lose its head or attempt to fight, as the men had done. It made itself at home. The cat found the Inspector's hat, stepped inside, curled itself up and prepared to go to sleep.

" You mustn't think I am a complete fool," said Jem harshly. He looked round at each one of us. His face was pale, but he was as defiant as ever. " I shall never admit defeat. You may have caught me for the moment but that will not be the end of it. Fools, you don't think I could run a show like this by myself? There are others, I tell you! Others, more powerful and more intelligent than myself. They will find means, they will make no mistakes. Above all," and here Jem looked at me, " they will keep themselves as hard as steel. They will not be soft. They will have no friends, love no man, have pity towards none. I made that mistake. But the group of men who supported me will not be like this. I have been weak, but they will be strong. You will not catch them like you caught me. They will have you in the palms of their hands. There are others, I tell you! Do you think I am a mad fool? I am saner than any of you. But it doesn't make any difference. I have failed. They will not fail."

And they took Jem out.

And I have failed, I thought. The police had brought a doctor with them, and while he was dealing with my arm, Charley looking down at me, cracking jokes, I was thinking how easy it would be to be glad. Had we not won? Jem was caught and there was no more danger. The doctors

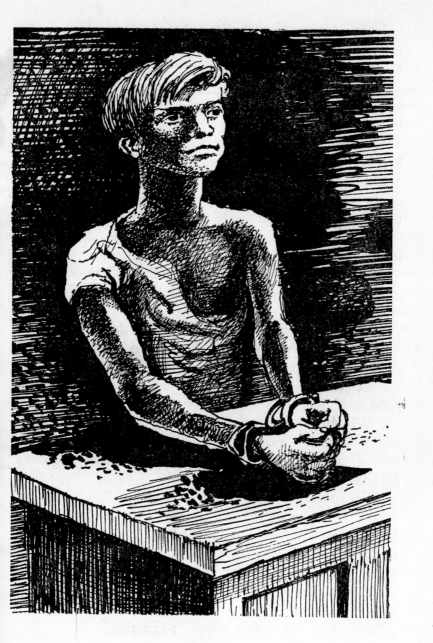

would find some way of giving their memories back to the townspeople, to myself, to Mr. Bowler and to Jack White. Why be gloomy then?

I think I took Jem's threat much more seriously than anybody else did. I could see, by the smile on the Inspector's face, that he did not believe what Jem said about the other men who would take his place. But I was convinced that Jem was telling the truth. I knew more than the Inspector, of course. I had seen the arrival of the ship and the unloading of the stores. I knew for a fact that behind Jem there must be many men and I felt cowed and alarmed at the thought we should have to continue the fight against them. It would be impossible to relax our vigilance for a moment.

But no, it was not entirely this fear. I had so wanted to defeat Jem myself, and Charley had taken the fight out of my hands.

I was lying on the bed in the sergeant's sleeping quarters. The bullet had been removed, my arm was in splints, and the doctor told me I should have to spend a while in hospital. He left me to deal with other patients. Only Charley remained.

"What's the matter, lad? Cheer up! You've done pretty well for a kid." He produced a pipe from his pocket, and began to fill it with some of the sergeant's tobacco.

"I'm fine," I said.

Jack White came in. He stepped over to the bed and looked down at me. He looked at my arm. He touched the knots over the splints. Gently, gently, like a woman's hands. I almost dared not breathe. "How are you?"

I had to ask him. "Jack, do you remember who you are?"

"No, son. The doctor's going to fix that."

That was enough for me. For that was everything. My little battle had not been in vain. The negro did not remember, but he was a human being, capable of love, capable of gentleness. Jem had been triumphantly defeated and I fell asleep.

CHAPTER XII

CONVERSATIONS WITH OLD FRIENDS

ABOUT two months later Mr. Bowler and I went for a
walk. When he was released from his cave prison,
Mr. Bowler had looked considerably thinner than
when he went in. His eyes were worried by strong sunlight.
But that was two months ago, and now he was looking very
sleek and gay, dressed in a very loud tweed suit, but nevertheless still insisting on wearing his faded bowler. He was
smoking a cigar. " See now, the beauty of nature," he said,
flicking the ash off the end of the cigar and waving his hand
towards the plum orchards, where the golden plums were
hanging like little lanterns on the trees. " Call me anything
but a tramp," he went on. " A tramp! What is a tramp?
A gentleman of the roads, a friend of nature, a happy man."

We had been very well treated. My arm was sound once
more, we had been given clothes, money, by the benevolent
society that had been organised to look after the afflicted
townspeople until they recovered their memories which, in
some cases said the doctors, might be quite a long time.

Mr. Bowler had come into his own. He had blossomed
like some magnificent flower, he used longer and longer
words, he stopped people in the street and presented them
with small gifts, wherever he went he was followed by a
small crowd of children who did not know whether to
laugh at him or throw stones. Then he would surprise and

delight them with a magnificent distribution of sweets. In fact, the way he lived caused a great deal of scandal. The managers of the benevolent society said that money had not been got together just for Mr. Bowler to waste in this extravagant way; and the best thing he could do would be to get some job and earn his living.

"Work," said Mr. Bowler grandly, "is vice. It has nothing to do with the art of living." Though when pressed to say what he meant by the art of living, he would become very vague, would say that it all depended what sort of a person you were, and wander off to gaze at the shop windows or lean on the river bridge where he held competitions amongst the village boys to see who could spit the farthest. Yes, there was no doubt that Mr. Bowler was getting quite a scandal and there was even talk of forcing him to work. What Jem had said had been perfectly true. Mr. Bowler had been a tramp and as a result of a series of inoculations that the doctors were giving us he could even remember patches of his previous life. On the whole, however, he preferred to pretend that he remembered nothing. He had become reasonably proficient on the tin whistle.

The managers of the benevolent society said that my education was to be taken in hand. They were going to send me to school. Jem had been careful to choose, at the beginning, victims who had few ties. It was discovered on enquiry, that I had none, no relations but an uncle, a shoe-maker, who had brought me up and did not greatly care for me. He had been quite relieved to get rid of me. I did not like the idea of being educated. I thought I could get on very well without it. My ambition was to be very much like Mr. Bowler. I thought of him as the happy man.

It was autumn. Wheat was golden in the fields and the grass-topped hills shone like mirrors in the still hot sun. But the swallows had already gone and other migratory birds were holding conferences to decide destinations and routes.

We left the town behind us and climbed the road in the direction of the sea. After a half an hour's gentle walking we caught glimpses of it. Mr. Bowler said that he hated the sight of the sea, and he was never going into another cave in his life.

But we were not bound for the sea.

There were many things I should like to have talked about, a number of things which I did not understand, all of them connected with Jem and the poison of forgetfulness, but when Mr. Bowler got talking these days, there was no opportunity to get a word in edgeways. He had enjoyed the limelight very much. He was pointed out in the street (so was I, for that matter) and loved it, beaming at the people who were staring at him inquisitively, raising his hat, and the final result of all this had been to send him sailing, like some romantic old galleon, into a summer sea of calm and fantasy. The sight of a penny bun in a shop window would cause him to make a speech. A plough team going across the rubble would awaken a poem in praise of labour. Children sailing matches down the flooded gutters during a rain storm would arouse his keenest interest and he would lean against a lamp-post with the rain dripping off the end of his nose, in order to wait and know the result of the race.

He could not think ill of anyone. Although he talked of nearly everything else under the sun, he rarely made any reference to Jem, whose trial was due to take place in a fortnight's time. Jem did not fit into the beautiful world that Mr. Bowler was allowing his imagination to make for him. He was being forgotten. The dark picture was being overlaid with brighter colours, brilliant reds and blues like the feathers of a tropical parrot. It was difficult to talk sense to him. If I asked him what he proposed doing in the future he would give an airy wave of his hand, light another cigar (he was presented with a box a week by an old lady in a neighbouring town, who admired him immensely) and say that when I grew up I should be an important man. " I am a failure," he said briskly and cheerfully as though this was the most magnificent thing imaginable. " You will remember me, no doubt, and despise me. Good! I don't mind." There was a twinkle in his eye.

It was quite late in the morning. We climbed over a stone stile and made our way diagonally across a field where sheep were grazing. The last time I had crossed this field I had met the eccentric old man cutting grass and his no less eccentric wife. Now shrill peewits rose and circled overhead.

" I hope we are not going to be late," I said.

" Impossible," Mr. Bowler said, giving the impression that time was measured not by clocks, but by his own coming and going. Whenever he arrived, that was the right time.

" All the same," I said, " I think we'd better hurry."

" What on earth is that noise? It sounds very distressing," he exclaimed, stopping short.

I thought it might be some creature in pain. It was obviously a big animal, a cow perhaps, who had been crippled by a fall. Whatever it was, the noise was coming from the other side of the stone wall which lay in our path. I ran on ahead and looked over. I withdrew my head immediately, and looked round in alarm.

" Well," said Mr. Bowler, puffing up—but I hurriedly told him to be quiet as we were in the greatest danger.

It was, however, too late. A round face surmounted by custardy coloured curls, appeared over the wall and

enthusiastically greeted me. It was the terrifying crimson
woman.

"You like my singing," she said in her bull-like voice.

"Who is this preposterous creature?" asked Mr. Bowler.

"I'd been wondering what had happened to you," she
went on. "We never see anything of you these days. Who
is this stupid looking man? Well, it doesn't matter. Takes
all sorts to make a world, I suppose. Come on over and
meet my son."

Mr. Bowler bubbled with rage. He would have made
some angry retort if I had not whispered to him that we
were probably trespassing on her ground, and that she
had a mad husband, who chased people with a scythe. And
then, aloud, I explained that we should be grateful for
permission to carry on with our walk as we were already
late for an appointment.

"Nonsense," she snapped. "Come and see my son."

There was nothing for it. First of all I helped Mr. Bowler to climb with a great deal of grumbling over the wall. I followed. On the other side was Red, his red beard neatly trimmed and a bright eager expression on his face.

"My mother was just singing to me," he said, a little unnecessarily.

"But you said your son was tall, broad, fair——" I began before I realised the rudeness of what I was saying.

"And isn't he?" she demanded. "A fine young man and for all the world like his mother."

There were never two human beings more unlike one another, Red, thin, short-sighted, and his mother, enormous and powerful. But I was very glad to see him under any circumstances. He remembered me very well, was responding to the doctor's treatment and very shortly hoped to be fully restored to his memory.

"Poor lad, he's mad," said his mother, "but when I sing it cheers him up amazingly."

The restoration of her son seemed to have sweetened the red woman. She insisted on our going to the farm for lunch but I said that we were very sorry, but we were already late for an appointment.

"I have an idea," announced Mr. Bowler, who had been carefully watching the woman. "If this lady and the young man would care to come with us we should be very honoured." The woman accepted enthusiastically on behalf of both of them; I felt that it would only mean trouble and was sorry that Mr. Bowler had spoken. On the way down the hill towards the coppice he confided in me, in a heavy whisper, that this was just the sort of woman that he admired. "A remarkable type, hot-blooded, passionate. What a colourless place the world is!"

As he made a great point of plying her with compliments, by the time we arrived at the gipsy encampment, they were the very greatest of friends. Mr. Bowler explained that farming was not the background for a woman of her obvious talents. He said that she was wasted in the country. In fact, he said, she was born in the wrong age. He saw her as some knight's lady, waiting for the return of her lord.

"Yes, I think I should have been pretty handy with a battle-axe," she said dreamily.

But in spite of Mr. Bowler's admiration, she was the very last person we should have brought to the celebrations that Charley was organising. I was so eagerly greeting Jack White, now looking more cheerful than at any time I could remember, shaking hands with Charley, who was sitting on the grass with his family around him, that I did not notice the ugly look that came into the red woman's face.

"So," she said, marching up to a turkey that was slowly turning in front of a wood fire. "That's where my turkey got to! Ah! you robber." She marched up to Charley and shook her fist in his face, "My potatoes, my turnips, my chickens. I'll have the law on you." In spite of Charley's formidable appearance (he was wearing an alligator skin belt, a purple shirt and a gallon hat) she would have closed with him there and then, for the only law she recognised was the law of her own right hand. But Mr. Bowler intervened and with a speech full of delicate flattery, in which he compared her to the goddess of harvest, pouring out riches for the children of nature, succeeded in making her sit down. He even asked her to sing. His victory was now complete. She smiled, ate an enormous share of turkey when the time came and said she was going to sing a love song for Mr. Bowler's especial benefit.

Fortunately, as soon as lunch was over she lay in the sun and went fast asleep. Mr. Bowler sat at her side, waving his bowler hat to keep the flies off her face.

" All the same," said Charley, " I don't trust her. It's just as well we're moving on."

" I'd like to scratch her eyes out," said Meg, dispassionately.

" Where are you off to? " I asked.

" Well, we've got set routes. Till Christmas we shall make for the east. We shall get sort of bedded down for the cold weather. Then, with the spring—well, that's a long time ahead, but we shall set ourselves up just outside one of the big towns. Got to earn a living now and again."

It sounded very attractive. I should have liked nothing more than an invitation to join them; Charley had invited Jack White to go along, and he had made no objection when Mr. Bowler announced his intention of keeping them company until he got tired of them.

" I'm coming with you," I said promptly.

" Oh no, you're not. Got no place for you, son," said Charley in a perfectly friendly way. " Besides, I should get run in. Got a serious sort o' police force these days, you know."

" See no reason why I shouldn't come," I could hardly get the words out.

" Keep your shirt on! Meg and me knows what's best for you. Know what you've got to go and do? Get a bit of education, then you can come back and talk business. Enrol you in the peg-making trade. Make you a master peg-maker." I knew he was laughing at me. I suppose he saw by the expression on my face what I was thinking and went to the trouble, and it was a lot of trouble, because it was a warm afternoon and we had eaten lots, of getting to his feet, coming and standing over me. " Them police would chase us up hill and down dale, into the sea and out of it. They'd get us. See? I like you."

So we said no more about it for the time being. The red woman woke up, sat up, yawned and before she knew where she was Mr. Bowler was kissing her hand.

As soon as I saw that I felt that this was no place for me. I wanted to get out of it.

" Fed up with us, aren't you? " said Meg.

" No, I'm not angry," I said.

She said that I ought to know better. If I kept my head screwed on the right way I should learn so much in the course of the next few years, that when the rest of Jem's pals came back, I should be ready for them. " O' course we know you're ready for them now. But you'll be better ready, if you see what I mean."

" You think there'll be others then? "

" Sure, lots of 'em. The best thing you can be about is learning and experimenting. You know, some sort of medicine that people can take so as this memory poison don't work."

" An antidote." Then I thought. " H'm! Not me. I'd rather stay here."

" A young lad like you too! Ought to be ashamed of yourself."

Before I went, Mr. Bowler came over and said that he would never forget me; on the other hand he said that he was not very optimistic about my remembering him. He said that we must not look on this as a parting. We were going to meet many, many times. Jack White shook me by the hand. They all, Charley, Meg, Jack White, Mr. Bowler and the red woman came with me to the edge of the copse.

By now it was quite dark.

" Not afraid of making the journey back by yourself? "
somebody asked me.

No, I was not afraid. I was not afraid of the dark.

Although there was a chorus of farewells I could not find
any words of my own and set off silently up the hill.

No, I was not afraid of the dark, I thought. What a
question to ask.

I heard somebody panting behind me. It was Mr. Bowler.
" A little gift, a parting gift, something to remember me
by. We were brothers in arms you know."

And he put his tin whistle into my hand.